"Hold leaving next to the drafty snack door. "Nothing's changed. Nada. Zip."

"I disagree. Everything's changed." His whole world had changed. Hadn't hers?

"I'm pregnant, not incapable of—"

"Just stop a minute."

Every emotion he'd buried for the past three years screamed to the surface. He pushed himself to his feet, struggling to keep steady, determined to keep his mouth and opinions shut. He couldn't. That was his child, too.

He leaned against the door, clawing his hair, indecisive. His attention was splintered between convincing Kate he couldn't protect her alone and protecting her himself by getting her into the mountains as soon as possible.

Kate constantly made him lose focus.

This time he had an opinion and she wouldn't change his mind. She…they—there were two of them now—needed protective custody. Maybe permanently.

ANGI MORGAN

PROTECTING THEIR CHILD

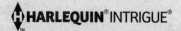

Cheers to "the magic room" and the countless twenty-minute sprints. A big thanks to Tenia, my mom, and Aunt Peggy for helping me work out the kinks. And a special thanks to Baxter, who said it was okay to blow up the chopper as long as he wasn't in it.

PLEASE RECYCLE
THIS PRODUCT IS RECYCLABLE

Recycling programs for this product may not exist in your area.

ISBN-13: 978-0-373-69690-1

PROTECTING THEIR CHILD

Printed in U.S.A.

H HARLEQUIN®
™ www.Harlequin.com

ABOUT THE AUTHOR

Angi Morgan had several jobs before taking the opportunity to stay home with her children and develop the writing career she'd always wanted. In a quiet house or traveling with her husband, she plots ways to intrigue her readers with impossible situations her characters may not overcome...until they find the one person who can help them for a lifetime.

Angi and her husband live in north Texas with only the four-legged "kids" left in the house to interrupt her writing. For up-to-date news or to send Angi a note, visit her website, www.AngiMorgan.com.

Books by Angi Morgan

HARLEQUIN INTRIGUE
1232—HILL COUNTRY HOLDUP
1262—.38 CALIBER COVER-UP
1406—DANGEROUS MEMORIES
1423—PROTECTING THEIR CHILD

CAST OF CHARACTERS

Cord McCrea—He is a sixth-generation Texas Ranger who transferred to west Texas to marry the woman he loved. He was severely injured in an ambush that was meant to kill his family, and has spent the past three years recovering physically and mentally.

Kate Danver McCrea—She divorced Cord and works her family's ranch. The last time she was in protective custody, two officers were murdered, she was shot and she lost her unborn child. The only person she trusts with her life—and the life of another unborn child—is her ex-husband.

Nick Burke—Kate's high school sweetheart who owns the neighboring ranch.

David Danver—Kate's father and owner of the Danver Ranch.

Ronald and Juliet Burke—Best friends with the Danvers, and the newest ranchers in Jeff Davis County. The Burke ranch shares a mountain border with the Danver ranch.

Mac Cauldwell—Former owner of the Burke ranch and now its foreman.

Shane and Sarah Boatright—Shane was Cord's partner. He and his wife were ambushed and killed by the Serna gang.

Jorje Serna—The leader of a Mexican gang being investigated for drug smuggling and other crimes in west Texas. He swore to personally kill Cord and everyone Cord loves after the Ranger shot Jorje's brother in self-defense.

Chapter One

"Your wife is a dead woman." Jorje Serna left the courtroom a free man, pointing directly at Cord McCrea.

The evil words closed Cord's throat in a moment of fear. A moment that pierced him as fast as the bullet that had broken his back. The ache around the scar was real enough. He recognized it. Fought it. Shoved it aside.

Free on a technicality after three years in prison, short years for the crimes Serna had committed. Incredibly long years while Cord's life as a husband and Texas Ranger unraveled.

"He's serious, you know." The lead prosecutor, Paul Maddox, tapped Cord's shoulder with one hand and dialed his cell in the other. "You and Kate should take extra precautions."

"Get her protection. The local sheriff can get to the ranch faster." Cord pulled his phone from his uniform pocket. "We may already be too late."

"On it. Go. You can meet them there."

Cord hit his speed dial as he turned toward the back stairs. "Come on, pick up."

No answer. He began running. Pain jarred him to a slow jog, and taking the stairs slowed him to a limp—the angle going down was torture.

"Kate. No time to explain. Get out of the house and call me."

He hadn't accepted a phone call from her in five months and doubted she'd reciprocate, but maybe she'd listen to the message. *Why?* You *don't*. That inner blabbing in his head kept at him until he pushed the exit door open.

The small county court appearance equaled close parking. Cord was in his truck within minutes of Serna's promise. Even at high speeds and running a couple of stoplights, he was at least forty-five minutes away from the ranch... and Kate.

Coming from a member of a vengeful gang with long tentacles in West Texas, Cord had no doubts the words were a serious threat.

He dialed his ex-wife's numbers again. Landline, cell, ranch foreman. No answers.

Cord wished the next hour would be the longest of his life, but it wouldn't be. He could recall every grueling minute after they'd been ambushed and shot. Each moment of his wife driving the opposite direction down this same road, yelling at him to stay with her, that he dare not leave her alone. Every tortured second of the next week as he mourned the loss of their unborn child.

Yeah, minutes crawled by, stuck in a hospital, unable to walk through a cemetery to bury your partner, his wife or your daughter. They completely stopped when he'd realized he could no longer protect Kate and must let her go.

The bastard Serna wouldn't take anything else from him. He flipped the radio on and listened, petrified he'd hear a notification by the Sheriff's department. Then he heard the dreaded words.

"Shots fired. Ambulance and backup needed at Danver Ranch."

Serna's men had probably been waiting at the ranch.

The truck skidded turning onto the gravel drive. Cord yanked the steering wheel the opposite direction, forcing the car to move straight. He punched the gas pedal to the floor. Sixteen minutes. That's as fast as he'd ever driven the private road to the house.

"Don't be dead, Kate."

Two cars, lights swirling on top, sat near his ex father-in-law's front porch. The closer he got, the worse the fear grew. He couldn't swallow. A fear he didn't understand gripped his heart and wouldn't let go. He slid to a stop, slammed the truck into Park and didn't bother to kill the engine or shut the door. "Kate!"

Two officers stood on the porch, one kneeling over an inert male, the other with his shotgun resting on his shoulder. He recognized Griggs, a deputy who'd been around the county five or six years.

"Where is she?"

"Shot this guy making a run for it from the house. He must have surprised Frank in the barn. We found him beaten, throat slit."

"Where is she?"

"No one else is here, Cord."

He recognized the voice of the guy kneeling, Sheriff Mike Barber, but Cord wasn't looking anywhere except inside the open door. "You're certain? Searched the sheds, the storm cellar?" he shouted over his shoulder.

"All clear. Car, two trucks still parked out back."

"No one took her? He didn't have a partner who may have abducted…" He couldn't finish the thought, but the horrific image of what Serna would do to her was already in his mind.

"Griggs came from the east and I came in from the west. One road in, McCrea, and it was empty." Barber had followed him inside the house. "Take a breath, Cord. She wasn't here. She's still safe."

"Serna seemed certain she was…that she'd been…" His

unsteady legs threatened to buckle under him. He locked his knees, standing next to the desk used by three generations of Kate's family for ranching business. "Were the ATVs out back?"

The sheriff shoved the curtains aside on the nearest window. "Only one. Do they have a pair? Is David Sr. in town?"

"Her dad's up with David Jr.'s family. Been there since a colt broke his arm in September." He might not talk to Kate directly, but he'd overheard his physical therapy doctor mention the break at the clinic. And how stubborn David Danver had been about resting the compound fracture. "It's possible she's out checking fences. Where does she keep that dang schedule?" He flipped through the stacks of papers. "Come on, Kate."

"Griggs, wait on the coroner," Barber called over his shoulder. "We'll take your truck, McCrea."

"Quickest way is the four-wheeler, Sheriff. Faster if I go after her. I can still find my way around here." He scanned the work schedule Kate's father had been meticulous about keeping. "Got it. Should be in the northwest quadrant today. I'll call as soon as I find her and get back into cell coverage."

"You sure you're up to it?" the sheriff asked. "That's an awful lot of ranch to cover."

"I got this."

He didn't wait for permission. He didn't need explanations of what had happened when the sheriff and his deputy had arrived. He didn't care. Serna's assassin was dead, but he'd send another. And another. Until Kate was dead.

It didn't matter to the gang that they were divorced. The soulless hatred Cord had seen staring at him throughout this week's proceedings confirmed that a war of sorts had been declared. A war that wouldn't end until Cord had been stripped of everything he held close and then was dead himself.

Revenge was a powerful venom. Since no attack had happened in the past three years, Cord had accepted Serna wanted it delivered in person. Damn all technicalities and the scumbag lawyers who found them.

He snagged the keys from the peg at the back door, along with a thick coat. Jumping on the ATV, he gunned the engine and shot around to the front yard to his idling truck.

"We'll be a while," Griggs said from near his vehicle. "Got an extra rifle in the trunk. Think you'll need it?"

"You never know." Cord cut his engine and retrieved his own 9mm from the lockbox under his seat. Grabbed his hat, cell and extra clips. "Make arrangements with Maddox for Kate's protective custody. I want her out of here fast."

"You got it. Hey, watch your back, McCrea. This guy came out the door shooting. We didn't have a choice taking him out."

"Thanks for getting here fast." He tossed his keys to Griggs and took the offered rifle. "Lock those inside the house, will ya?"

"Anything for you guys."

Cord knew that look. Pity. He'd faced it for the past three years. Everywhere he went in town, all the interviews and therapy sessions to make sure his head was screwed on straight. How could it be? He'd lost his unborn daughter and his wife. Nearly lost the use of his legs, his job, his life.

He straddled the seat, powered up again and left before anything else could be said. It was easier to leave with a curt nod of acknowledgment. After about a year he'd learned what to say to get around the questions. Learned how to avoid the dialogue.

At least with everyone except Kate.

He couldn't fool Kate.

He couldn't protect her before and now she was in danger again.

"No more!" he shouted down the trail, to God and any-one else who could hear. "This is going to end!"

TODAY WAS LIKE every day on the ranch but then it wasn't. Kate McCrea finished the repair on the barbed wire, picked up the tools and put them back in the satchel on the four-wheeler.

She'd grown up stretching and repairing fence, taking care of the stock, cleaning and cooking alongside her mom for a houseful of men. Not that her brother didn't have to jump in and help with the biscuits or bacon.

The thought brought a smile to her heart and curved her chilled lips. A welcome change after the week of tense up-dates regarding Jorje Serna's appeal.

Working the fence was solitary and peaceful. Lord knows she got enough of that around the house, but it was different with nothing else except the base of the Davis Mountains in sight. The wind was the only roar in her ears. No airplanes, no tractors, no whine of the refrigerator driving her crazy.

Silence.

Completely interrupted by a racing engine heading to-ward her. She missed using horses to ride the fence, but they'd made the switch like most ranchers.

"Dang it, Frank. I told you I could handle this today." She complained into the chilling wind, watching the ap-proaching four-wheeler bounce across the pasture a little faster than usual.

With her extra scarf wrapped back around her neck, she pulled on warmer gloves, shoving the worn leather work pair deep into the pockets of her work coat. "Gosh darn it, I really wanted to be alone."

He must have news about the trial since she was explicit about her return to the house. She'd had a feeling when Jorje Serna's case had been accepted for appeal that he'd be released. His threats scared her to death. Frightened her enough to consider leaving the ranch. But the only way to keep her father from mending fences with a broken arm had been to send him to her brother in Colorado.

She debated whether to go or stay every day.

Especially now.

She had another life to think about. Even through the thick jacket she could feel the small swell to her belly. She wouldn't be able to hide it much longer. Her family knew and she'd be forced into a face-to-face confrontation with Cord soon since he wouldn't return her calls. Even their lawyers couldn't get a response.

She couldn't believe he knew and had rejected them. No matter what had happened and the chasm that had grown between them, they were going to be parents. In spite of their differences, he was a good man. Stubborn, silent, stoic… but a good man who would be a great father.

The far pasture had been perfect today for thinking. Pondering big decisions and the advice from everyone who wanted to help. It was up to her, though. She was alone with this decision, especially since Cord wouldn't talk to her.

The sting of tears heated her eyes and cooled her cheeks. Too often, too fast and too much out of her control. She turned back to face the mountains, swiping at the tears, getting herself in hand.

The engine grew louder, idled a moment and cut off.

"What's happened?" she asked.

"Kate?"

Cord? So Serna had been released. That was the only reason he would come here. Today. "Frank shouldn't have told you where I was."

"Kate, Frank's dead."

She couldn't move and grabbed the fence post for support. "Serna?"

"One of his people. He was released going on three hours now."

"I'm surprised he waited this long to make a move." She wiped the tears for Frank off her face. The last time she'd seen Cord she'd been crying, silently watching him stand in their doorway as she drove from the house. She refused to face him again still falling to pieces and pushed her sunglasses into place. There'd be time for tears later. "Frank was a good man. He'll be missed."

"Kate—"

"Don't. Let's just get back. I have to call Dad and the guys. How soon can we have the funeral?"

"You won't be here."

She couldn't avoid looking at him any longer and couldn't believe what he was insinuating. "I'm not leaving everything and running away."

"Protective custody isn't running, Kate."

He was closer than she had anticipated. Only a couple of steps separated them. His six-foot-two shadow fell across her eyes, thankfully hidden behind dark glasses. He couldn't see her notice how lean he'd become.

He'd traded out the Ranger hat for his favorite Stetson, held now in his ever-polite hands. His hair was department-regulation short, just like when they'd met, fallen in love, married and been happy. Completely different than their last night when she'd shoved her fingers through the longish length. The day before the divorce.

No matter what the circumstances, watching him stand on his own two feet gave her a lump in her throat. "I see you're back in uniform, but you need to remember you can't tell me what to do anymore. We're not married."

"I could never tell you what to do, babe."

Habit. Wanting to run to the protection of his arms was

just a habit that needed to be broken. *No sniffles. Stand strong.* "Let's go. I have things to do."

She stepped toward her ride and his hand wrapped around her upper arm. *Keep it together.*

"I mean it, Kate. I can't protect you and take out Serna." *He's going to kill him.*

"First off, I can protect myself." She pulled her arm free. "And you can't possibly think you're going to win this thing. Are you planning a suicide run to 'take out Serna,' or depending on another verdict that's supposed to keep him in isolation the rest of his life so the rest of his gang doesn't come after us?"

She threw his words back at him. She'd known Cord for seven years, been married to him for five. The determined angle of his head slightly cocked to his right, that sharp-angled nose of his pointing over her shoulder. Straight, full lips pressed flat across his teeth. All signs he was making a stand.

Was he even aware his body shouted his intentions? She knew him better than he did. His nonanswer confirmed her fear, adding fuel to the apprehension she'd been fighting all week.

"Dad blast it, Cord! I'm not going into protective custody. There are plenty of places I can be safe. Davy's house in Colorado is a fortress."

"It's temporary. Maddox is arranging it."

"And are you going?"

"We don't have time to argue." He snagged her arm and gave a gentle tug. "Come on."

"No." She yanked free a second time, stepping back out of his long reach. "I'm not going anywhere until you give me your word."

"It's the only way you'll be safe."

"Like Sarah and Shane? Like a week after you were in the hospital?"

A direct hit below his belt. She knew it was a low blow as soon as the words spewed from her fear. He felt guilty enough and none of it had been his fault. He'd just been doing his job.

Both Rangers had been with their wives when the double ambush happened three years ago. Shane and Sarah never had a chance against Jorje Serna when they'd pulled away from their favorite restaurant. Serna's younger brother had caught her and Cord on the ranch drive, shooting Cord before he returned fire and killed him. It was still hard for her to make the drive to town without reliving that traumatic emotion.

The wind whistled through the tall brown prairie grass, vibrating the fence wire, echoing the void that had grown between them. There was so much they'd left unsaid.

"I didn't mean that." She advanced a step toward him but he backed away before she could touch him. "You have to believe that I don't blame you."

"Not a problem. Let's get out of here."

She'd known the dangers of his job when they'd decided to marry. "I didn't mean to lash out, but I won't trust the police with my life."

"Shane and Sarah were ambushed just like us. This is different."

"Not really." Her hand went protectively across her belly, always remembering the feeling of emptiness after losing their unborn daughter.

Cord was face-to-face with her in a blink of an eye. She couldn't back away again. In spite of everything, she needed him. She felt so all alone.

"Trust me, Kate."

His touch, wiping yet another tear from her cheek, forced

her to look closer at him. The strain showed in his eyes. The hurt she understood too well. There was so much to say....

And if she were in protective custody, the words would never happen. There was no guarantee when she'd be back or if she'd ever see Cord or her family.

"No. I'll go to Davy's. He can send someone to get me."

"Dammit, Kate. This is not the time to be stubborn."

"I've made up my mind." She climbed on the four-wheeler. "No more discussion."

"You aren't going back to the ranch house then. It's one thing leaving with security, but you can't wait for David Jr. to come collect you at a place Serna's already attacked. Successfully." He pulled his cell phone from his shirt pocket. It was the first time she noticed that he actually had her father's work coat on. "Just verifying there's no coverage."

"I have a hand radio, but if Frank's—"

"Right. No one's listening at the ranch. So we punt. We'll spend a couple of nights at Caliente Lodge until we know for certain when your transportation is showing up. They have a working ham radio up there, right?"

"I assume so. The guys check it out every fall when they restock the supplies. They went up three weeks ago. We'll have to have horses to get up there."

"Horses at the line shed?"

"When have they not been?"

"Who's there?" His eyes were scanning the horizon. Making certain no one had followed him?

"Juan."

"I'll take the lead. When we get there, Juan can take a message back to Griggs or Maddox with the new plan." He swung his long legs over the seat as naturally as mounting a horse. No awkwardness from a man who couldn't walk two-and-a-half years earlier.

"No chance you'll change your mind?" he asked in his deep, low voice.

"None."

"We're taking a huge risk getting to the lodge." He replaced his hat and shoved the top closer to his ears.

"I know, but if we leave now, we'll make it just after dark. Cord?" He acknowledged her with a pause while buttoning the jacket. "Your word, please."

"Want a Scout's honor, too?" He started his four-wheeler.

"Just your promise. And I know you were never a Scout."

"No protective custody." He revved the engine, obviously angry. "I promise." As soon as the words were said, he shot forward in a cloud of dirt and grass.

"I promise, too, kiddo." She tilted her head, comforting their unborn baby. "I'll keep you safe or die trying."

Chapter Two

Even on ATVs, the trail to get the horses took a little over an hour. Kate's back killed her from the bouncing around, but she knew it didn't hold up to the pain Cord must be experiencing. He stopped once to make certain she was okay and she could see the strain on his face. The wheels were chugging along behind those dark brown eyes in that investigator-problem-solving mind. After seven years, parts of him were obvious. Or so she thought. Some stayed completely hidden.

The Cord McCrea who couldn't walk for eight months. *That* man had shut himself behind a door she'd never been able to open. One who she'd waited for, given up on, and two years later finally asked for a divorce.

"Is that Juan's truck?" he asked, stopping and killing his engine just out of sight of the line shack.

"It's Dad's old Chevy."

He stiffly climbed off the four-wheeler and pulled his weapon, checking his ammo. "Keep your rifle ready to fire, Kate."

"You can't possibly think someone's beat us here. How? There's nowhere to hide a car and it takes much longer than an hour to drive. It's safe."

"Griggs had to kill the man who shot Frank. There wasn't a vehicle. And it's been closer to three hours since that happened. Took me a while to find you." He dropped his hat on the seat. His familiar short hair barely had a dent from the impression. "Didn't take much training to see the man wasn't alone. I didn't get a look at Frank, but I can't imagine they were able to pound your whereabouts from him. But we don't know. Too many uncertainties. If you won't go into protective custody, then we trust no one and take nothing for granted." He nodded to the rifle strapped behind her. "Get it ready and stay out of sight."

He darted into the brush and the sparse trees. She followed him with her eyes, unable to look anywhere else. She didn't hesitate and followed his instructions to unstrap the rifle, bringing it across her knees. She wasn't leaving the ATV, though. It was her only means of escape.

"You've made me a paranoid scaredy-cat, Cord McCrea," she said to the wind.

Prepared, not paranoid.

There was a difference. The security detail assigned to protect her had gotten lax after eight days. Both men had lost their lives because they hadn't been prepared. She might not agree with his orders, but she'd brought the rifle and two boxes of shells with her on the chance Serna was released today. Prepared.

"Shoot, Frank. I sure wish you'd heeded my warning. I'm sorry you died because of me," she whispered, and dropped the sunglasses into her pocket, pushing away more tears that blurred her vision.

The minutes ticked slower and slower as Cord crept closer to the line shack. One room with one door, one window, one cot and an outhouse that she needed badly. What was she doing? Risking everything on a man who had mentally walked away from her and wasn't approved for active duty, that's what.

She stood to watch him check out the shack by looking

through the window. The door opened and Juan stepped outside. Cord waved her forward.

"Guess that was the all clear." She replaced the rifle, fingering the safety back on. "I know, baby. I might as well face that it's going to be a rough couple of days. Maybe years."

She pulled up in front of the shack just as Juan was pulling away in the truck.

"Where's he rushing to?"

"I filled him in and sent him back with a message for Maddox." He stretched his back and started down the dirt ruts they used for a road.

"Wait, I can take you back."

"We're not staying, but it might be better to put out Juan's fire and eat the chili he told me about."

"You sure you can make another two hours on a horse?" His back must be cramping; her muscles sure were.

"You paid a lawyer good money not to worry about me anymore, Kate. No reason to start again."

Probably to prove a point, he took off jogging over the rough terrain. The man wouldn't let her see him limp. Nope, he would never be vulnerable. Not with anyone and especially not her.

"Okay." She sighed. "A very *long* couple of days."

"THE HORSES ARE SADDLED." Cord entered the shack, tossing his hat in the corner at the foot of the cot. When he turned to unbutton David's coat, he finally caught a glimpse of Kate. "What the...you're...you're pregnant?"

"Obviously." Kate pointed to her belly, showing beneath the tight layer of thermals.

Jealousy shot out from his gut, twisting Cord's insides. Was it someone he knew? Jenkins had helped her while he'd been in rehab. He knew Nick helped her at the ranch. Had she gotten back with her old boyfriend? God, please don't let it be someone he knew.

"Why so surprised? When you wouldn't talk to me, my lawyer sent you a registered letter. I explained everything."

He commanded his voice to remain steady, no inflection, nothing accusatory. Hard to do when you're thinking of your wife with another man. *Ex-wife*. "Who's the lucky dad?"

"Really, Cord? Was your phone off for five months and three days?" She sighed, extended and heavy with exasperation.

"But that's the day we...the night before the divorce?"

"That's right." She raised her chin just a hair and compressed her lips. "Mr. Sixth Generation Texas Ranger Cordell Wayne McCrae is..." She paused, and her bottom lip began to shake.

"A father?" he finished for her.

His legs wouldn't work. He took a step toward her, but the wobbly things wouldn't hold him upright and he knew his body sort of hit the door and slid to the floor, even though feeling really hadn't set in.

"Cord!"

Kate was closer. His hand smacked the bed on the way down and his hat fell to the floor beside him. A soft hand swiped his face, a strong one shook his shoulder.

"Are you okay?"

"I'm great, just tripped." The fall added another bruise to his wounded pride. "I was sort of surprised."

"So surprised you fell down."

"Why didn't you tell me?" Dad-blasted humiliating sticks for legs were tingling under him like they were asleep.

"Think about the hundred or so messages I've left for you, Cord. You never listened to any of them?"

"I couldn't." Meeting her perfect sky-blue eyes didn't work. He was ashamed of himself. She'd needed him and he hadn't been there. Hadn't been for three years. "I had no idea that's why you were calling. This changes everything."

"Hold your horses, cowboy." She stood, leaving him next to the drafty shack door. "Nothing's changed. Nada. Zip. I'm still going to Davy's."

"I disagree. Everything's changed." His whole world had changed. Hadn't hers?

"I'm pregnant, not incapable of—"

"Just stop a minute."

Every emotion he'd buried for the past three years screamed to surface. He pushed himself to his feet, struggling to keep steady, determined to keep his mouth and opinions shut. He couldn't. That was his child, too.

He leaned against the door, clawing his hair, indecisive. His attention splintered between convincing Kate he couldn't protect her alone and protecting her himself by getting her into the mountains as soon as possible.

Kate continually made him lose focus.

"You promised." She divided the chili into two bowls already sitting on the two-foot log table.

It had always amazed him that she could hold an argument or discussion or share intimate stories while prepping dinner or making a bed. Even trimming trees. She just pushed right through whatever she was doing, barely pausing for responses, just expecting a nod or acknowledgment that he was listening. This time he had an opinion and she wouldn't change his mind. She…they—there were two of them now—needed protective custody. Maybe permanently.

"I promised before I had all the facts. Completely voids the agreement." He stated the facts. How could she be so calm about having a kid?

She's had five months to get used to the idea. He had less time to think about it before the baby arrived.

"You can't pull that reasoning on me. I thought you knew

about the baby." Her movements might have reflected ordinary things that needed to be done to eat, but he could see the strain, the tension just under the surface.

"I didn't."

She stood straight, faced him, tummy between them. The urge to pull her close had his hands tangled together behind his back to stop himself. *Are you happy?*

"Nothing's changed. It's still safer to get me—" she put her hand over her small belly "us—to Davy's than anywhere else. All of us, even you."

"No."

The one word shooting across the room caused her shoulders to drop and had her sighing in disappointment. He knew all her sighs. A habit she'd tried to break for years but could never conquer. Her eyes dropped to his hands when he removed his gloves. He should have taken off his wedding ring long ago. Somehow, he'd never felt comfortable without it on. He pulled it and shoved it on his right hand.

"And that's your final word? You won't come with me?" she asked, seeming fairly certain of his answer.

There wasn't a choice for him. No options. No way out. "I'm not leaving this unfinished." *Not again.*

"It's suicide."

She was right, but he had to protect his family. He hadn't before, but this time would be different.

"We better hit the trail before much longer."

"I'm hungry and not going anywhere while there's a drop of this chili left. Juan's a pretty good cook. He must have made this at home to bring with him. So sit down, enjoy it as much as possible and rest your back. I know it's hurting."

She was right. Dang it. The muscles were aching like an entire string of curse words. He hadn't favored it, so how had she known?

Hell, she always knew. Nothing ever got past her.

They both sat at the small table tied together with horsehair. He leaned over it, sitting in a stiff bodark chair while she sat on a mattress that he knew was very comfortable.

Didn't matter if Juan was a good cook or not. He couldn't taste a thing. His memories had him twisting in his seat and he wasn't likely to enjoy anything. They'd experienced several nights on that dang mattress.

Several nights enjoying the rustic line shack far from cell reception, from last-minute on-call duty or surprise leads in the investigation. He was headed for a tailspin if he didn't block those thoughts. Wouldn't look good to walk it off outside since she'd just let him know he'd be a father.

Sheeze...I'm going to be a dad!

Unable to speak or actually think of anything appropriate to say, he spooned several bites of chili into his mouth hoping not to choke. He hadn't thought he'd ever be around Kate without thinking of her as his wife. And he hadn't accomplished that task yet. One of the reasons he hadn't listened to messages or opened envelopes was simply to stop thinking about her.

Stop thinking of the long, silky curtain of hair draped across his chest when she rested her head in the perfect spot. A spot she'd taken months to find so she could stay in his arms all night.

What happened with them now? Was he supposed to ask? Was it too soon? Was he supposed to tell her how happy he was at the thought of being a dad? Or how terrified he was that Serna would take her away from him permanently?

Push the emotional subjects aside. He had to clear his head and decide what they needed to accomplish today. First priority, get Kate out of here...alive.

"You know I hate it when you call me Cordell." He blew on the chili and shoved another couple of bites down.

"I still think it's funny how upset you get at Chuck Norris's character having the same name. As much as your dad pretended to dislike that show, he watched the reruns every day. You should be honored he was consulted about it."

"I know."

"Did you ever order him the DVD set like we'd talked about?"

He put a bite of chili in his mouth and shook his head.

She set her bowl on the table and leaned back against the wall. Sighing. A short one, mainly through her nose. And, yeah, he knew how to interpret that one, too. She was ready to talk and let him have it for not visiting his father. She probably knew he hadn't really seen anyone except the shrinks and physical therapists for close to two years.

"You haven't talked to him, have you?" she asked.

"Don't start, Kate." He knew she knew the answer. They'd been together too long. Or *had been together.*

She crossed her arms and tipped her chin into the air in a determined show of downright stubbornness. She was about to let him have both barrels. Then all her reasons and frustrations—whatever they were—would tumble out. He'd listen and wouldn't interrupt since she'd be right. Then it would be too dark to leave till morning. And then they'd be sleeping here on that one mattress. 'Cause he was certain he wasn't sleeping on the cold, drafty boards forming the floor. No, sir, now wasn't the time to hash out how stunted his emotions were.

Remind her how dangerous the situation is.

"Don't get me wrong, Kate. I know there's a lot to talk about. Now's just not the best time." He dropped his spoon on the table. "Serna probably has someone watching the ranch house. The longer we stay here, the more likely the bastard will get curious about why we're not heading back. Hell, he might already know where we are 'cause Juan showed up."

"I understand all that. I didn't say a word. And it's amazing how you can't unless you're issuing orders." She grabbed her bowl and ate.

The silence grew.

He turned his bowl up to his lips and spooned what he could in his mouth, chewing the rest as he stood and stretched his aching back. This afternoon had been the most activity outside of physical therapy that he'd had in three years. He was not looking forward to a couple of hours on horseback over rocky terrain, in the dark.

"Leave the dishes in the well bucket. I'll put out the fire."

She didn't argue, just dropped the metal bowls with a clunk into the only water inside the shack. He pulled the extra blankets off the shelf, rolling them tight for their saddles—just in case they didn't make it to the cabin.

Man, he needed the dad-blasted water to put out the fire.

Slow on the uptake. That's what he was. She'd known and that's exactly why she hadn't made a different suggestion. He might be a Texas Ranger, investigating drug cartels and other illegal activity, but his wife would always be a whole lot smarter.

KATE'S FAMILY HAD kept the line shack simple. She loved the hand-assembled furniture put together from boredom by ranch hands over the years. Some of the cast-iron pots had been used on cattle drives a century ago. There was no way she'd let it rust. She scrubbed and oiled the old Dutch oven while Cord made a trip to the well to water the horses they'd leave behind.

Keeping it simple kept the shack an unattractive place for people passing through their property. Nothing of real value to steal or carry off. Her family and all the ranch hands had to accept the fact people were going to cross the land. There was a lot of acreage, making it impossible to monitor one hundred percent of the time. A plus on their side was that the land wasn't desirable for much.

It had only been in the past five years that they'd cleared and widened the trail so a vehicle could drive here. About the same time they began utilizing ATVs. That was a long and muscle-aching project. Every free day Cord had off from duty that summer was spent moving rocks and smoothing the road. Her dad had loved how his son-in-law had just assumed he'd be there to help.

Kate swiped the back of her hand across her eyes. No crying. Nope. Nope. Nope. There were things to do and definitely places to go.

Everything was stored. Supplies were sealed away. She pulled her sweatshirt on and packed herself in her winter garb. She'd just stepped out the door with the rifle when the muffled sound of an engine caught her attention.

Then it was gone.

She ran the short distance to the corral and opened the gate. She didn't have to see a vehicle to know whoever had driven up wasn't on their side. Whoever "they" were, they had stopped far enough away to hope for a surprise attack. She pulled the cinches and shooed the extra horses into the open field.

"Kate." Cord's voice was deep and low, barely audible. "You ready?"

She slid the rifle into the center of the blanket he'd already tied to the back of her saddle and stepped into the stirrup. "I am now."

His arms were right behind her, circling both ends of the saddle, his body close enough to touch her leg. She wished she could brush his smooth cheek with her fingers. His left hand landed on her thigh and gave her a comforting pat. "Stay low and get out of here as fast as possible. Don't look back."

"I'm not leaving you behind." She pulled tight on the reins, holding the sorrel under her in check, searching Cord's eyes to see if he was saying goodbye.

He'd done that before and she'd refused to let him die on her.

"Leave. Your job's to protect the...the baby." He tapped the horse's rump and she skittishly jumped forward.

One last look at the father of her child, then she clicked at Candy and they flew.

As fast as her horse could cover the hills stretching in front of them, she put more and more distance behind her. The riding was hard. Slumping low in her saddle wasn't the easiest, most comfortable way to ride. How she wished she'd heeded Cord's need to hurry. What price was she going to pay for the foolish sentimental value of a Dutch oven?

"Come on, Candy girl, get us out of here."

She heard the pop. She knew what it was. Knew the long echo of the sound bouncing through the low hills to the far canyon walls. She'd heard it for the first time when she was six years old and her father had taught her which end of a gun was what.

She waited.

"Come on, Cord."

Candy kept moving forward, and Kate twisted in her saddle, looking.

No one followed. Then, after what seemed an eternity... more gunfire.

"Daddy's alive, munchkin. Just delayed while he kicks some ass."

Chapter Three

No fire. No camp. No Cord.

Kate searched behind her, confident that Cord could follow the trail she'd left. If he were following. If he weren't injured. If he weren't dead.

"Dumb, Kate," she whispered, her breath forming a little fog in front of her. She couldn't let herself think that way. Of course Cord was on his way. He'd make certain he wasn't being followed and when he saw the trail veer off, he'd make certain no one else would see where he'd headed.

The clear, beautiful night did nothing to calm her nerves. Stars shone in the midnight black, but not having even a sliver of the moon made seeing difficult. She took a deep calming breath of chilled air. She'd done it a thousand other times during her life in West Texas. Just like camping, riding, shooting and waiting.

She should have stayed to help. But the scared look in Cord's eyes made her let him jump into action while she ran. He wasn't thinking of himself, just her and their child. What if…

"I will not let my imagination run all over the country. He'll be here," she whispered to the baby, her hand searching for it under her coat. "He'll know where to come."

Deviating from the plan to go to the lodge seemed right. Once the gunfire stopped, she couldn't bring herself to potentially lead anyone following her straight to the only safety net they may have left. They needed that radio. One night in the open cold couldn't kill her, but being trapped by Serna's men certainly would.

Candy whinnied. Short and sweet, as if calling to another horse. Kate quickly stood, pulled the saddle girth, draped the reins over the sorrel's neck and mounted. All the while searching the darkness for a white Stetson. The rifle was in her hands, safety off before she thought twice. She heard movement just below her, but still couldn't see anything—or anyone.

She'd chosen a spot a horse couldn't reach easily. Familiar to her and Cord. He'd proposed here. Under the stars, a brilliant, clear summer night that seemed lifetimes ago.

"You really need to stop talking to yourself." Cord's voice cut through the silence. She saw his short brown hair pop up behind their rock. "Heard you clear at the bottom of the trail."

She dismounted Candy and looped her reins around the bottom of some scrub, keeping the rifle in her other hand. Not wanting to talk about her concern for his safety. No matter how much she still cared for Cord, they couldn't be together. "You all right?"

"Yeah, just sore. Lost Griggs's rifle on the rocks. He's going to be irritated."

She didn't need much light to see his pinched expression, the tightness in the way he moved, the slowness of each step leading his horse, Ginger, up the steep slope.

Cord plopped down on a smooth surface. She stuck her hand out for Ginger's reins and he couldn't raise his arm.

"What happened? Where are you injured?" She quickly staked his horse, clicked her safety on the rifle and knelt beside him.

His hairline was covered in sweat as if he'd been running,

which she hadn't seen since before… Well, running wasn't a plausible explanation when he'd brought a horse. He might say he was fine, but he couldn't hide that he was in pain.

"Don't lie to me, Cord. We'll get through this situation—and stay alive—a lot faster if we agree to just say what we mean and be honest."

"Okay." He unbuttoned her father's work coat, pushing down the left sleeve.

"Were you shot?"

"Not hardly. You know, for some would-be assassins, those guys stink. Couldn't hit the shed or a moving six-two target."

She searched his arm and each movement caused a grimace. "There's no blood."

"I tripped. Wrenched my shoulder out of place."

"We need to get you to the hospital."

Cord looked at her like she was from a different planet. His lips compressed as if he were gathering strength or holding back his real opinion. "What we need is to get to the cabin and the radio. We're one hour ahead. Two if we're lucky. I slowed down two of them, can't guarantee they aren't out of the picture permanently. The other two left in the Chevy."

"Dad's truck?"

"Right. Juan's either working with them, or they were waiting for him. Either way, we can't risk going back to the ranch. You have to help with my shoulder, babe."

Her heart did a little flip at his endearment while her stomach churned at having to pop his shoulder into place. *God, give me strength.*

Juan working with Serna? Juan telling Serna they were headed to the cabin? A two-hour lead? Frank dead? No one knew where they were? The thoughts shot through her mind at lightning speed, but why had her sure-footed, boot-wearing ex-husband "tripped"?

"You're not talking."

"I'm concentrating, trying to remember the last time, if ever, that you've tripped." She pulled her gloves off, dropping them to the ground. "I also have a very vivid memory of the last time I tried to pop your shoulder into place."

"Right after the touch football game on the Fourth of July in Valentine."

"As I recall, it didn't turn out well and you spent three days in a sling." She shoved his coat off his right shoulder with just a bit too much enthusiasm and he growled. "Sorry."

"I understand why you're angry."

"No, you don't. I don't understand, so how could you?" It was natural to care about the father of her child. The tension from the past several hours hadn't lessened just because he was safe. She had to think of what would happen next. And she might be a little bit mad at herself for not having thought about anything except Cord. "Let's just fix your shoulder and get out of here. Okay?"

Drops of sweat beaded on his brow. She wanted to gently wipe them away, take him to a doctor and…and… She shook her head and swiped the stones from directly behind Cord.

She pulled her jacket off and laid it behind him, along with his own. The ground was uneven and rocky. She'd been shifting on it for an hour waiting on him to arrive and knew how uncomfortable it was.

"Lie down on your jacket and walk me through this. I've never done it correctly before."

He caught her wrist in a solid grip. "Kate. I'm sorry you worried."

Did he really think that's all it would take for her to forgive him? They were so past those words. Stupid hormones caused her to consider just how sorry he was.

"You ready?" she asked. *Please don't let me mess this up.*

He lay back, his voice strained as he told her step-by-step how to put his shoulder back in its socket. An old injury from before she'd known him. A bad fall in a college football game. Tech vs. Texas maybe? That's all she knew. He rarely talked about his past and she'd most likely heard a version of the story from his father or mother.

A solid pop, a loud grunt through clenched teeth and Cord rolled to his side away from her, holding his shoulder.

"I'll make a sling from a blanket."

"No." He gulped a couple of times and stood, rotating his arm, the pain clear with each forced movement. "No time. Let's hit the trail."

"We can wait a few—"

He took her shoulders in his strong hands, jerking her to a stop. "Serna is determined to kill you, Kate. He wants to take you from me like I took his brother from him. Believe me. There's no stronger motivation for revenge. We can't wait around. I need to get you out of here. The faster, the better."

"Still no chance you're coming with us?" She knew the answer before she saw the look in his eyes.

He understood revenge. He wanted it for Sarah and Shane and even a daughter he'd never held.

Cord turned to his horse and rested his head on the saddle a couple of seconds before lifting his hand to the saddle horn and pulling himself up top. He had to be in terrible pain, but they'd gone through worse.

Much worse.

"THERE HAS TO BE ASPIRIN or something around here."

Kate had been opening and banging cabinet doors for ten minutes. Cord didn't know how to calm her down. At least he was consistent, 'cause he'd never known what to do or what to say.

"It's okay, babe. Come on, sit. Rest a minute."

"Stop telling me what to do and definitely stop calling me 'babe.'" She wrapped her arms around her middle, giving herself a hug, and crossed the room to the rocker.

He couldn't start the lodge generator. They wouldn't be able to hear anyone coming. So they were wrapping up in heavy blankets. Fortunately, there were flashlights and extra batteries so they could at least see a little.

"Wish I could start a fire for you. You've been cold a long time."

"Don't worry about me." She rocked furiously, determined in whatever her thoughts were at the moment. She blew on her hands, rubbing them about as fast as that rocker was rocking.

"Why don't you catch some winks. I'm not sure how long we can stay. If they followed—"

"There you go again." Rocking, she threw a hand in the air, waving at him as if he knew why she was so totally out of sorts. "There weren't any horses for them to follow with. And since we didn't come back, don't you think that Maddox and the Sheriff's office are just a bit curious as to why? Don't you think we have till morning to make a decision?"

"I was just making a suggestion, ba—Kate. I'm sort of tired myself."

"Then *you* take a nap."

"I'm not the one who's pregnant." That must not have been the right thing to say.

"Men." The one word ended on a long huff.

Man, he needed aspirin. Not only was his body rebelling at the fall and horseback riding, his head ached from trying to keep up with Kate.

"Do you mind getting me the small Philips head? Remember where the tools are?"

He remembered. Tools were in the bench seat by the front door. Extra blankets in the cupboard between the bedrooms. Towels on the shelves above the bathtub. No hot water unless the generator was running or you heated it up in the cast-iron pot in the fireplace.

The cabin looked the same. Simple. Clean. Neat. No real valuables. No personal mementos since multiple families used it year-round. Fewer people during the winter since the road wasn't easily accessed and ended four hundred feet below. It was officially on Danver land, but could only be reached by car from the ranch to the northwest, Nick Burke's place.

Kate slowly stood, wrapped a blanket around her shoulders and sat at the table in the corner.

"This dang radio should work. We should have already sent a message to my brother or father, who would be rallying the troops to get here. We should have notified Maddox about the attack. What's wrong with the stupid thing?"

He handed her the pouch of small household tools. She was crying, swiping at tears of frustration with the back of her hand. What were you supposed to do when your ex-wife cried? Comfort her? Keep your hands to yourself? Definitely keep your hands to yourself. Except this woman also carried his child. The situation was complicated so he kept his hands on the flashlight and the beam of light where she was working. Ignoring how upset she was, ignoring how he felt.

Department-forced therapy had made him think. As much as he wanted to shrug suggestions and thoughts away, he couldn't. If the shrink didn't approve him service-ready... he'd be behind a desk for a long time. So he'd recently been thinking more about the past three years than he wanted.

Watching Kate get more upset and frightened brought each of his wrong turns into his mind, but he couldn't see the solution.

So he held the flashlight.

"Why does every plan we have go wrong? This should have been a safe way out." She unscrewed the back panel of the radio. "There's no way to fix this—it's missing tubes. The hands didn't say anything about needing parts or I would have ordered them."

"Who brought up the supplies?"

"Juan and Bernie."

"Juan again. Something doesn't feel right, Kate. Serna's men couldn't have predicted that we'd come here. Why sabotage the radio? Is anything out of place?" He searched the neat room with the limited lit view. Nothing seemed wrong.

"Honestly, I don't know. I haven't been here since that last time with you. Don't go jumping to any conclusions. I just haven't had time and there hasn't been much of a reason to lately." Her hands protectively caressed their child. "We rarely use this place anymore. Dad hasn't hunted since Davy left home seven years ago."

Before, he would have come up behind her, slipped his fingers through hers and just stood there, holding and loving her. He'd thought that had been enough. Guess nothing was enough when you couldn't defend your family.

"Tear the place apart. The radio parts have to be here." *Or something else showing us what's going on.*

They searched. Methodically. Silently.

Beginning with the east side of the cabin, they opened each door, taking everything off shelves, checking the backs of closets and the pantry. He searched the fireplace, the pot-bellied stove, the mattresses for new threads or lumps. Each quarter hour he swung outside to look and listen. Nothing and no one.

Cord's back ached, reminding him he needed to stretch it out flat and relax. He couldn't. He had to be missing something.

"There's nothing here," she said, putting her hands on her lower back and stretching side to side. "I'm exhausted."

"It's after midnight. With no radio, we should ride down to the road, cross over to Nick's place and make arrangements for your dad to come get you. You catch some rest on the couch, I'll wake you at first light. And that wasn't an order, Kate."

"I know. I'm just cold and tired."

She was right. Serna's men would have already been here if they'd had access to horses. And if they'd determined they'd gone to the cabin, a little smoke wouldn't alert anyone. He brought in more wood and, without any discussion, lit a fire. The living area warmed immediately. He pulled the couch closer and Kate snuggled beneath several blankets.

The thought of warming his wife—*ex-wife*—throughout the night made all the aches take a backseat to the craving his body had for her. But he was a McCrea and could keep his distance, even if that meant holding Kate tight.

Determined to do what was needed and not what he wanted, he grabbed a pillow off the bed, switched off his flashlight and waited for his body's need to defuse.

"Promise me it'll work out," she said softly from the couch.

"I promise." *No matter what needs to be done. I promise.* "Move over."

"What? Why?"

"You know why. It's in the teens outside, not too much higher in here. It's a lot warmer on the couch than on the floor. I gotta be able to move tomorrow."

"I don't think that's a good idea."

"It's the only option. Now move over."

She crowded to the cushions, tucking a blanket around her back. If he'd wanted something to happen, that thin layer wouldn't stop him. He was more concerned with keeping her warm, relaxing his back and listening for signs of Serna's men.

"Good night, Cord."

He may have grunted a bit when she shifted once or twice. Her breathing steadied and she was out within a couple of minutes. Something she'd always been able to accomplish. She told him it was her clean conscience. If that were the case, no wonder it took such a long time for him to fall asleep.

THE FIRE HAD DIED DOWN.

4:00 a.m. He'd dozed. Last time he'd looked at his watch it had been just after two.

He shifted away from his hold on Kate, reluctantly removing his arm wrapped around the baby. Good Lord, she was pregnant again. He pushed the thoughts of three years ago away, burying them deep so he could think how to get them to safety and keep them that way.

Sitting on the hearth, he dropped a couple of logs on the fire, building the heat back up, casting a glow across the most beautiful woman he'd ever known. Her pale yellow hair seemed to sparkle as much as her eyes when she was ticked off at him. He could think of a couple of times her anger and frustration had actually turned into a nice romp on a bed, or whatever else was handy.

The thought made him laugh out loud but didn't wake her.

The cold, flat floor called to his cramping back.

He checked the horses through the window, examined the open terrain as much as possible in the starlit night. Nothing.

Why not come after them? What did Serna know that he didn't?

Cramp. Floor. Stretch. Relax.

When the pain had subsided to a dull throbbing, the fire popped, drawing his attention. Cord looked at the back of the old couch—or under it. The boards where the heavy log frame had been sitting were uneven.

"Right under us the entire time." He pulled the bench seat open and grabbed the ax. Using the blade he pried the wooden floor panels loose.

"What did you find?" Kate aimed the flashlight where he worked.

"I'm not sure, but I think…"

Sticking his hand under the boards, he didn't have to search long before his hand snagged a large bag. He knew without looking it was drugs.

He popped up more and more of the loose floor.

"Oh, my God, Cord."

"There are at least twenty bags here. Serna's men made use of your family's absence. This is the perfect place to hand off drugs to suppliers without authorities close by watching."

"How long do you think they've been using it?"

"How long has Juan been an employee?"

"At least five years."

"I bet Serna's been laughing at how close I was to everything and could never gather enough evidence for a conviction. Dammit, we stumbled right on top of his operation." He could beat himself up later. He opened a large bag, shoved a smaller one into his pants pockets and began replacing the boards.

"You don't know how long this has been here."

His gut knew. Serna had taunted their investigation by keeping the drugs under their nose. Then ambushed their families to get them out of the way. "We need to get everything back to exactly where it was."

Kate laughed. "Sorry, what do you think they'll do if they discover we know? Try to kill us?"

She had a point, but it might buy them some time. Either way, she folded the blankets and put things in their place. He finished the floor and moved the heavy furniture back, even moving the dust around so they couldn't see the drag marks.

"If they assumed we were coming here…" Kate hesitated while dousing the fire. "Do you think they've created another trail this direction that we didn't see in the dark?"

"Worse."

Cord held her jacket and she slipped her arms inside. "I don't understand."

"We had suspicions that Serna's operation was using planes to get drugs farther north. Flying under the radar so they couldn't be tracked."

They left the cabin, not trying to hide their presence, but at least it didn't look like they'd found anything of importance. The horses were rested enough for a trek to Nick Burke's place. If they pushed hard, they could get there late tonight, but it would be a difficult ride, no stops, out in the open. Plenty of places a chopper could fly in low and pursue them.

"There's no way Serna could have built a landing strip without us knowing," she said, once they had their saddles and gear packed.

"It's wide open for choppers, babe." They both swung onto their horses' backs in time to see the first edge of pink on the horizon. "Five will get you ten, they have ATVs hidden somewhere nearby to get them in and out fast."

"If they do, there's only one place they'd be able to hide something that large." She clicked to her horse and took off away from the trail, toward the ridge. "We'll get to Nick's a lot faster on ATVs and they'll be on foot."

"Kate, no!" He clicked his heels into the horse and caught

up quickly. "We can't look for a drop zone or four-wheelers. That canyon is a three-sided death trap for us."

"We're sitting ducks on horseback. You know that. It would be safer doubling back across our land than getting caught in the open. Those ATVs would catch up with us no matter which way we choose. This is the only logical thing, Cord."

Smart woman. Too smart for her own dang good.

"Logical doesn't mean the safest." Like that would deter her once she'd thought it through.

"I'm not changing my mind. We can find those ATVs or whatever they use." She didn't slow her horse, either.

"I can't allow—"

She turned in her saddle to face him. Old jacket, beat-up scarf wrapped around her neck, determined look in her eyes piercing his heart.

"Don't say that, Cord. This is my fight, too. It always has been."

Chapter Four

Galloping with the father of her child. It should have been a pleasant experience, not a petrifying one. He shouted again and she pulled on the reins to slow a bit. The terrain demanded a slower pace. Cord wanted her to stop, talk about what they'd do, think about their options. They didn't have any options. They needed to beat a chopper to the nearest landing site.

Thinking that idea was possible seemed completely ridiculous. They'd be outmanned and outgunned. But if the two of them could get there, they'd have surprise on their side. She was certain it was the only way. And certain that Cord would find a way to deter the men wanting them dead.

One thing about riding at this speed and direction, it didn't lend to much chatting. It took a lot of concentration. Cord was more of a doer anyway. She'd always liked that about him until the shooting. A piece of him had shut down and never come back to her.

With each hint of sunshine peeking over the hill, she heeled Candy just a little faster. It was a risky gambit. One she needed to play if her family was going to survive. She couldn't live fearing someone waited around every corner. She didn't want to live constantly wondering if Serna or his gang members would make that day her last.

"Come on, Kate! It's too dark to be taking the trail like this," Cord shouted from behind her.

Thank goodness the path wasn't wide enough for the horses side by side. If she looked at him...well, she just wouldn't look at him until it was too late to back out.

"Kate! Think what you're doing!"

"I'll wait for you at the vista," she shouted over her shoulder. The wind was so strong she'd be lucky if Cord understood anything. She reined Candy off the trail leading down the mountain and headed for the closest place this high a helicopter could land. Slowing over the rocks for the horse's benefit, she was still way ahead of Cord.

To her knowledge, her ex-husband hadn't been on a horse since the shooting. And he'd never been on Ginger's back, so he couldn't be certain of her abilities.

Cord kept within shouting distance. Probably mad, but he followed. He didn't have an option, since Kate knew he'd never leave her unprotected. They may be divorced, but he was an honorable man. Sometimes too honorable.

It would be so easy for Kate to push Candy just a little harder and leave Cord in the dust. This ride in the dark was dangerous as it was without her ex-husband getting more worked up. Candy broke through the scrub and they were in the open at the edge of the incline. Down into the box canyon or around the top of the ridge.

"Are you crazy? What if you'd fallen? Or your horse had stumbled, sending you into the rocks?" Cord's deep voice stated on an offended breath as he pulled Ginger to a stop.

Her heart still raced as fast as the horse's. She dismounted, looping the reins around some juniper. Cord was one step behind her, fisting Ginger's bridle in his hand.

She turned to face him, completely uncertain about the next step and totally unwilling to acknowledge his worry.

"What do we do now? How can we stop these guys? You're trained for this, right?"

"All of my training told me to head to Nick's, not into a gunfight or barreling down a dark trail with a pregnant woman."

Uh-oh. That's why he'd been shouting. Sometimes she forgot she was pregnant. The doctor said to go through her normal routine, normal exercise, and that riding—within reason—was good for her. "I got it. Sorry."

"Can you see anything?"

Cord wasn't looking along the horizon. His search was below them, in the small canyon—if it actually qualified as one. Kate followed him to the edge of the rock face and searched. "I can only see two possibilities. If they've hidden ATVs or a vehicle, they'd be closer to the rocks. But there aren't any caves in this area to hide anything."

"There." He pointed to an unnatural outcropping of rock. "At first glance it looks like part of the sloping wall, but it's not. It's been camouflaged."

"You're right."

"Gotta be a vehicle of some sort under there since I don't see any fence or hay for horses. Will you let me handle this alone?" he asked with a quick look at her belly.

"No."

"I didn't think you would." Cord looked away, seemingly focused on the fake rock lean-to.

"Someone needs to have your back." She watched him stiffen as he stood taller. "I mean, I should help. You shouldn't do this alone."

"You're right. I'm heading down the rocks and you stay here to cover my back. I'll need eyes up top."

He faced her, one straight brow slightly arched. She could see the triumph in his eyes. He'd tricked her. She'd demanded to help and he'd agreed and kept her up here out of the way.

"Just because I'm pregnant, doesn't mean—" Her first instinct was to argue, but he was right, she did need to think of the baby. "Okay, I'll be your eyes. What's your plan?"

"Shh. Do you hear that?" His hand cupped her shoulder as he froze.

The distant whomp-whomp-whomp of a helicopter bounced around the hills and she couldn't discern which direction it came from.

"No time for discussion." He shoved the reins in her hand and handed over his hat before skidding down the hill in his boots. "Just stay here. No matter what!"

Five minutes. They needed just five lousy minutes to beat those murderers.

"And just how am I supposed to warn you if anything goes wrong?" She raised her voice, confident no one else was there yet. "Wait, Cord! Maybe we should go straight to Nick's?"

"Keep those horses out of sight."

Where? The juniper trees were a bit thicker behind them where they'd ridden, so she backed them up and tied Candy in place. She wouldn't go anywhere, not with a saddle on her back—she was too well trained. Ginger was her exact opposite and would bolt at the first distraction, so she took her scarf and covered the horse's eyes. She headed back to the ridge with her rifle and extra shells in tow.

While moving the horses, she'd lost sight of Cord. She'd seen the evidence that his back was hurting him with every movement, but he hadn't let it slow him down. Neither had his shoulder. She lay on the rock path perfectly still and watched the lean-to. She pinpointed Cord by seeing his arm a couple of times outside the camouflage. If she hadn't known he was there, he would have been invisible.

Hopefully, someone else would have to look twice to see either of them—her dirty work coat was the same color as the red-and-brown stone but her hair... She pulled her neon-colored knit hat off and stuffed it in her pocket. She'd been hunting enough to know how to blend into the scenery. She pulled her pocketknife and whacked the bottom of some brush, shook off any attached critters and set it over her head to hide the blond.

What is he doing?

Helicopter sounds grew louder. It must be flying close to the ground. She couldn't see it, but that was the logical assumption. It shouldn't be there and no one had reported seeing or hearing one to her. Then again, if Cord's insinuations were correct, Juan might have been coordinating arrivals with the dates he was at the line shack.

The helicopter topped the vista and swooped over the edge with a practiced flair. It swirled around, sending dust and small rocks in every direction. Tiny whirlwinds of dust shot into the air near Cord's location.

I need you alive, Cord.

THE CAMO HID more than just the gang's transportation. Cord discovered a small man-made cave where supplies and gas cans were stashed. Sheeze, there was even a table and chairs. For what?

If they used the cabin, like he suspected, then why a second unloading area? One look at the box contents and the pieces of a five-year investigation were beginning to fit together. He heard the chopper landing and squeezed his sore body uncomfortably between the rough rocks and a couple of crates marked Hazardous.

Cord had suspected that Serna's gang must have used the cabin for years. It was Serna's style. Break the law in plain sight. It's exactly why he'd shot Kate himself instead of sending minions. And why he'd gone to jail. But he and Kate had stayed alive for three years. Cord half expected, half hoped for the gang leader to be on that chopper.

This could end real fast if he was.

Stuffed like a sausage behind the crates, he couldn't see a dang thing outside. He could hear a guy complaining about unloading the chopper by himself. Heard the whine of the chopper blades slow to a halt. Several Spanish curse words mumbled loud enough for others to respond and tell him to stop his whining. At least three men, two most likely ready for an attack, covered the one unloading.

Four to one.

And him in a cave. All they had to do was wait for them to leave. Kate would never wait. She'd fire and take at least one out, one would keep him pinned down, and another would go after her.

You should have just slashed the tires.

Then there would be no doubt he and Kate were close by. What could he do?

Gas cans.

Lots of gas cans!

It was risky. A logical assumption that they'd fill up the ATVs before heading out. He inched the crate toward the cave entrance, just enough to give him room to dive for protection. Waiting for unloader man's return to the chopper, he quickly moved, unscrewed the lids of the front two gas cans and scooped handfuls of sand inside. One good shake and he was set.

Back behind the crates, he waited for the next trip and repeated the procedure with the next two cans in line. Then he moved farther away to wait.

Please wait, Kate. Be patient.

CORDELL MCCREA, WHAT are you waiting on?

He couldn't get out without being seen. How was she supposed to warn him after they'd already landed? She couldn't. He'd known that.

Rifle ready, she slid along the path until she lined up a better shot. She'd have his back…and his front. Her daddy had shared his gift of being a marksman.

"Ouch. Shoot." A piece of dried cactus had lodged itself in her jacket, and one of the thorns had stuck through the material and scraped the skin of her arm. She hurriedly knocked it away with her hand, catching another thorn in her thumb. She'd known better but just wasn't slowing down to think. She wiggled her fingers, attempting to keep the tense nervousness in check.

The pilot stayed put while three men jumped from the chopper, ducking low with the blades still rotating above their heads. One had a rifle leaning on his chest. The other two headed straight for Cord.

Any second.

Nothing.

Where had Cord gone? The man with the rifle stood at the helicopter like nothing was wrong. Voices, strong, angry words in Spanish. The pilot was still inside, but the blades were slowing—he'd cut the engine.

Four to two. Not such bad odds.

Could she do it? Could she shoot a human being?

The picture of Cord's bleeding body rushed before her eyes. He had bled from multiple bullet wounds these men— or men just like them—had put there three years ago. It was hard to forget him attempting to say goodbye to her while rushing him to the hospital. Instead, he'd coughed up blood. He'd come so close to being killed by those monsters.

Yeah, she could defend Cord and their child. She funneled her anger into concentration. She took aim, keeping the barrel trained on the man with the gun who seemed to be searching the rim. One man unloaded boxes from the rear seat, disappearing under the camouflage.

If she could take out the one with his finger on the trigger of a machine pistol first, the odds might be better for keeping Cord alive.

Still nothing.

Kate only had a clean shot for the guard. She couldn't act with Cord trapped wherever he was hidden. So she had no choice but to wait, hoping and praying that the men in the helicopter were the only ones around. She was a sitting duck for anyone approaching behind her.

A clear day with lots of sunshine. She'd soon be a little warmer lying on the cold, rocky earth. If they could time this correctly, the men would be completely blinded by the sun rising over the rocks.

Maybe I should have talked things through with you, Cordell.

The men unloading and seeming to gripe about every trip back to the helicopter finished and chugged bottles of water. It wasn't hot, but in the high desert most kept themselves hydrated. As thirsty as she was, she would not move until Cord was out of that canyon.

The pilot finished whatever he'd been doing on the opposite side of the helicopter. The echo of him slamming something back in place bounced around while he wiped his hands and wandered to stand by the guard. He shoved the red work rag in his pocket, elbowing the assault weapon slung across his back, out of the way.

Still no sign of Cord or that he'd been discovered. There must be a cave entrance hidden by all that camouflage.

What were all the supplies for, and if they had this place, why use the cabin to hide the drugs? These men were packing weapons ready for a battle. They didn't need to be good shots with machine guns. Just point and shoot. Both she and Cord had limited ammo but were excellent marksmen. And they still had surprise on their side. That had to be in their favor.

Outgunned and outmanned. Yeah, I should have talked through some plans with Cord. What did I get us into, baby?

Chapter Five

Desperate times called for desperate measures.

He'd heard that saying throughout his lifetime. Each member of his family had bragged on how they'd made it through the Depression, more than one world war. Men and women had sacrificed so he could walk the land he worked every day.

This barn had been erected by his father and fellow ranchers. A monument to the prosperity of the times. The tack room had been his refuge growing up. Now the whole place housed more broken-down junk and car parts than horses. And at the moment, Serna and two of his men.

It didn't matter how bad the situation had become, no one from any part of his life would approve of the lethal men he was "in bed" with now. Drug gangs. Murderers. Men who didn't think twice about taking a life and leaving the body somewhere to rot.

He knew the risks. He also knew what would have happened if he hadn't agreed. *He'd* be one of those bodies rotting somewhere to be discovered by a stray desert hiker.

He watched Serna's show from the corner of the tack room, careful not to turn his back on his partners of the past four years. Hopefully, they didn't notice how tense he stood waiting to be spoken to. Probably never noticed that he kept his .357 shoved under a pile of broken harnesses, easily within one step.

Watching this gang leader lose control reminded him of what type of men his "business" partners were. He didn't trust any of them and wanted out. Hell, he'd never wanted in. Another saying of his grandmother's popped into his head. Bargain with the devil—or his agents—and you're gonna get burned. But that was the price you paid when things were going belly-up and there were no options left.

"They couldn't have disappeared. I told you, they were going to that thing they call a lodge," Serna spit into the cell. The newly released state felon ranted, waving his arms in his sharply pressed stripped shirt. Ironic that the stripes were heading the opposite direction than the prison bars he'd been wearing until yesterday.

If McCrea was at the lodge, he wasn't worried. He hadn't wanted a money trail and had accepted payment of another kind. His personal stash of heroin was hidden but no one had found it for four years. Nothing to pin him to the gang once he got rid of the burner phone.

"I told you McCrea is the number-one priority. Doesn't anyone listen to me? No! Bring him to me alive. I want to rip his head from his freakin' Ranger's neck and spit down his stinkin' throat." Serna clicked more buttons and finally slid the new phone into his back pocket.

He stood there. Waiting for Serna to state what he needed.

"Those incompetents working for me will receive the same if they don't find that cowboy and his whore soon. The entire schedule will be thrown off. They should have waited and taken them all out at ranch."

He waited for one of Serna's men to answer or explain why that had been impossible after Serna had threated Mc-Crea at the courthouse. No one dared.

And neither did he.

Serna might not kill him, but pissing him off right before this last shipment wasn't part of the plan, either. Making a boatload of money and blaming someone else—the Danvers were as good as anyone else. *That* was the plan. And if poor little Kate got caught in the crosshairs again...so be it. No skin off his nose.

"What? No one feels like talkin' to me," Serna declared with no question in his angry bellow.

"We're waitin' on orders, Boss," one young man in the back sheepishly mewed.

"I order you out. Go! Leave!" Serna touched the handle of his pistol tucked in the front of his pants.

The lead minion couldn't find the door handle fast enough before the four men bunched to a stop trying to figure out how to get out. Serna threw back his head, laughing. The heavy wood swung shut on its own accord.

Serna sauntered toward him. "So cool. Never acting afraid."

He stood in his corner, forcing his expression to remain the same. He shifted his weight closer to his weapon, itching to take it and shoot the scum dead. But he was a necessary evil to finish his plan. He'd dealt with middlemen while Serna had been in jail. Things had gone easier after Serna had gone to jail and vowed to kill McCrea. On a personal level, he only wanted the Ranger out of the way so Kate would be gone, too.

Dealing with this mad dog in front of him had grown tiresome fast. Mad dog? Yes. Continuously high on a cocktail of drugs, consistently popping more pills. It was amazing Serna had ever accomplished any type of workable drug smuggling across the border. And nothing on the scale of what they were attempting.

"Do I have a reason to fear you?" he asked more coolly than he'd thought. The sweat under his arms and the line gathering to trickle down his spine physically showed the truth.

"My friend…"

I'm not your friend.

"Things have been going good, yes?"

"I'm not complaining."

"Did you know about the little—" he pursed his lips together and shrugged "—shortage I was told about last week?"

"No shortage. You were told where the drugs are. We thought it better not to go in so close to your hearing." *It was also part of the plan.* "We'll move it with the rest."

"Then why not continue our arrangement? So much time and energy wasted finding a new route."

"You know why, *friend.* The DEA is getting too close for horseshoes and grenades."

"They haven't discovered us in four years' time." Serna's eyes were dilated and when he faced the early-morning sunlight, he pulled his mirrored shades to his nose. "What makes you so certain that they're getting…closer."

The drug addict patted his shoulder in a demeaning way, fingering the grip of the gun at his waist. Trying to command the situation. Serna had no idea he'd been used in this carefully constructed relationship.

When the DEA found the cave—and they would find the cave—the gang would take the fall. A means to an end to restore his financial stability. An end he'd wanted for many years.

I'm a small pawn in the overall picture and Feds will love to give me immunity for what I know about your organization. Serna, you are so screwed.

He wanted to shout the truth. Wanted to bark it back at this doper just what kind of a mistake he'd made forcing him into this situation. He kept his voice low and calm, saying, "Let's get this shipment taken care of and worry about the rest later."

It was dangerously close to the time hands would begin showing up for work. Should Serna be reminded he didn't want to be seen here by anyone? Five more minutes and he'd have to tell—or ask—him to leave.

"I agree, *amigo*. But first, we take care of our runaway couple. Edward!" Serna faced the door, waiting on one of the men to reenter the room. "This is exhausting for me."

"You need something, Boss?" The youngest, who'd dared to speak earlier, kept one foot out of the room.

"Time to get moving." Serna spoke more Spanish, lower, loud enough only for Edward to hear, nod and leave. "Mc-Crea will be found and dealt with. You're certain they'll head across the mountains?"

"Everyone knows David's at his son's place. If they need help, that leaves the friendly neighboring Burke ranch. We wouldn't be looking for them if your guys had taken them out at the shack."

The look of hatred on Serna's face accentuated the prominent lines of droopy skin, the yellowish tint of his eyes. He wasn't healthy, but of course, he was a drug addict of the worse sort. The question wasn't his physical health...just his mental. Was he stable enough to finish?

"Do not piss me off, *amigo*." Serna paused his exit, slowly sliding his arms into his jacket, always playing the role of some huge crime lord. How laughable.

His jaw popped as he gritted his teeth, his eyes narrowed to slits. "Nothing else matters to me until that bastard is dying a slow death while he watches me kill the one thing he loves more than his own life."

"I have no problem with that. If McCrea's alive, the operation is at risk."

No problem at all. He was only here for the money.

Chapter Six

Cord had never been good at waiting. For months doctors and physical therapists had instructed him to be patient. Don't rush things. Don't push his legs too far. Even his father and mother had warned him.

The minutes ticked by. No one reached for the gas.

His legs cramped. The shaky sticks weren't one hundred percent. He hadn't passed the physical test to requalify but none of that mattered. If he failed, Kate would die.

Their child would die.

So to quote whoever said it first, "failure was not an option."

Option one—sand in the gas tanks, seize up the engines. ATVs couldn't follow when they rode out on horses. Chopper still could. He'd take out the pilot or engine with rifle cover.

Then run to the top of the ridge? On these legs?

What was he thinking?

Option two—shoot everyone. There couldn't be that many—they'd come in a chopper loaded with extra weight. Three or four men tops. What type of weapons did they have? Was Serna with them? Could he even get to the entrance without being seen?

I'm blind in this cave.

Option three—wait. Not his favorite option. Kate was

most likely going nuts on the rim. Would she wait? He'd reminded her of the baby; maybe she would listen this time.
Unlike getting out of the car when they'd been ambushed
three years ago.

Damn...not now.

The memory of the shooting rushed into his mind. Once
there he couldn't get away from it. It was so real, taking
over his optic nerves and replaying in slow motion in front
of him. He saw the gun barrels. Heard the shouts to shoot
Kate. Yelled at her to get down. He turned to protect her....

Searing fire in his back, then nothing.

Kate screamed, kept screaming his name. He could still
move his hands, his fingers still gripped his weapon. "Roll
me over, Kathleen."

She'd nodded, the fright vivid in her beautiful, tear-filled
eyes.

"Wait until he's on top of us," he whispered.

Concentrating only on Kate's face, he'd stayed conscious
for her. She rolled him. He'd ignored the pain but could remember it now, wincing at the vivid memory. Then he'd
squeezed the trigger, shooting Ronaldo Serna between the
eyes. The second man with him must have been stunned,
pausing just long enough for Cord to get a second shot off,
severely wounding him.

No repeat performance. Kate was screaming now. She
was up on a ledge waiting for him. He would get out of this
bear hole without being shot. He wasn't doing that to Kate
or his child. He just needed options.

A real shot echoed through the box canyon. Men scrambled. Bullets connected with metal.

Kate hadn't waited. Or she'd waited long enough. He
rolled over the crates and prayed his legs wouldn't buckle
when he hit the earth floor. They held and he shoved his
back to the wall at the cave entrance.

First guy through the entrance he coldcocked in the face. Out cold on the rocks.

Second guy backed through the entrance, tripped over the body of the first and raised his face into the barrel of Cord's weapon. He raised his hands in the air, letting the machine pistol hang across his shoulder.

"Drop it."

The guy shrugged.

"Don't let the uniform fool you. This is personal and I'll drop you like the jackal you are. Now take the strap over your head and stop pretending you don't understand."

The man complied and Cord kicked the gun into the sunlight. He used his belt to immobilize the man's hands and feet and dragged him to the back of the cave by the gas cans. He lacked time to do anything else. He slung the machine pistol across his chest and positioned himself behind the ATV. Still hidden to the chopper pilot, he heard Kate's rifle between the rapid firing of another automatic.

There were shouts in Spanish calling from the chopper to the cave asking where they were. The gunfire didn't stop. From his view he couldn't find Kate on the ridge.

ONE LONE SHOT pierced the silence and then nothing.

"Cord!" Kate shouted. "Are you alive?"

"I'm good." He kept low to the ground and zigzagged to the chopper.

"Good. I think I...I killed him." Her voice shook—he could hear it even at this distance. "He's not moving. I haven't seen him move."

One glance at the pilot and he didn't need to take a pulse. He'd been shot in the throat. He waved his arm at Kate. He still couldn't see her. He couldn't find the fourth guy. Where had he run? And if the man had heard him shouting at Kate...

Rapid gunfire from the cave took down the pole and the tarp collapsed. He fell flat and used the chopper as cover. The edge of the tarp dropped and blew across the ground, but bullets pummeled the rock face behind him. He lifted the machine pistol and pulled the trigger, hearing his own spray of bullets bite through the camouflage. A short curse and then silence.

They'd broken free inside the cave, found another weapon and now were dead. He checked the bodies for a pulse. None. And no ID. Where was the fourth man?

"What the hell does Serna have planned?" No more time to search the crates. He had to find that fourth guy. They needed to get out of there and fast. It would take them several hours to get to Nick's without a vehicle. They could have used the water for the horses, but he had no way to carry it up that ridge. They'd have to take the trek slow, hiding their movements.

When he edged from the cave, he saw the bastard picking his way to the top of the ledge.

"Kate!" he shouted, running to the bottom of the trail.

Maybe she'd seen him, couldn't get a shot from her angle with the rifle. Cord aimed the MAC-10, squeezed the trigger on the inaccurate weapon and nothing. The magazine was empty. He wasn't close enough to use his 9mm so he had one choice. Climb.

The steep incline he'd used before would be easier but longer. Straight in front of him, there wasn't a path, but the incline wasn't completely perpendicular. He could get there before the fourth man.

He pushed hard. No sound from Kate. His blood pumped hard from the strain. Little sleep and hours on horseback had taken its toll on his body, but he pushed up the hill, shouting for Kate and not receiving an answer.

A cramp seized his back. He bent forward, stretching

and praying for it to end. He had to get back to Kate but he had to stop this man first. He pushed harder and evened up with the man on the side of the canyon. He ran toward the guy, ignoring when his feet slipped on the uneven hill. The small pebbles were dangerous, but he dug his boots into the soft earth, maintaining his balance.

As soon as he was in range he pulled his weapon from his waistband. "Hold it."

The fourth man pivoted to escape.

"Come on, man, you've got nowhere to run! Drop the gun."

Fourth guy stopped, began turning, but his hands weren't in the air. Cord dropped hard to his knees, steadying his weapon. The fourth guy began firing as he turned. Cord pulled the trigger, hitting his target and planting his face in the dirt until the machine pistol was silent.

He looked up in time to see the fourth guy tumbling down the incline to the canyon floor below. The body rested at an odd angle and didn't move.

Even if he had time to check the crates or hide the bodies, he didn't think he could make the climb up again. He had to think of Kate. No more delays.

His body felt as tough as a marshmallow. He took the remainder of the easier trail as fast as his wobbly legs would carry him.

"Kate?" She didn't answer. He knew what was wrong as soon as he topped the ridge and saw her lying on the ground. She was still under a bush, still gripping the rifle, finger still on the trigger. Her grip released as soon as he touched the barrel. She covered her face with her hands, dropping her head to the dirt.

She'd shot a man.

Dead.

Cord stretched out beside her, pulling her to him, ignoring the rocks, his shaky muscles and his sore shoulder. Even ignoring that he hadn't held her in his arms for five months and how much he'd missed her.

It wasn't about him.

She'd just killed a man.

"Kate, honey, you did what you had to do. Those men would have killed us."

"Is he really dead?" she asked between soft hiccups.

His Kate always got the hiccups when she cried.

"Don't lose any tears or sleep over this guy, Kate. He's not worth it."

"Every life is worth it, Cord." She shoved him an arm's length away. "*Every* life."

"Go ahead and get mad at me if that's what it takes." They sat up, shoulder to shoulder, looking toward the high plains and Davis Mountains. "You can't be certain it was your bullet. Could have been mine."

"You were firing?"

He hadn't been. He'd never admit it, but nodded affirmation.

"I thought…before it all happened, I was so confident. I didn't think I'd…but when he turned toward you, I couldn't just watch you get shot again." She dropped her face back into her hands, drawing her knees to her chest. "I just couldn't go through that again. So I pulled the…you know."

Cord watched the little involuntary jerk her torso did when she was holding in the hiccups. He'd always thought it was cute before. Had teased her about it relentlessly. Now all he could do was rub her back.

"You did what you had to to protect yourself and the baby."

She hurried to her feet, heading down the trail where she'd hidden the horses from view. Cord followed.

"So how do we get down to those ATVs?" she asked.

"We don't. We're stuck on horseback."

"I don't understand." She dusted off her work pants, stowed her rifle and adjusted her saddle.

"I put dirt in the gas." The trail was narrow and he passed on the opposite side of her horse, removing her scarf from Ginger's head and hanging it across Kate's saddle.

"You put—dirt, huh? I don't guess you've learned to fly a helicopter in the past five months?" She tugged Candy's cinch tight and rested her forehead against the leather. "You were going to wait it out, weren't you? If I'd known, I wouldn't have started shooting. If—"

"Don't do the 'what if' thing, Kate. They would have left someone behind. The results would have been the same. You saved my life." He heard his shrink's voice rolling inside his ears. *Admit your mistake. Maybe it will help.* "Okay, I was wrong for not having a plan before I took off."

There, he'd admitted his feelings out loud.

"You certainly were." She looked down on him from high on Candy's back, having mounted while he had his back turned.

"Wait a minute! Aren't you going to admit that *you* were wrong for getting us into this mess?"

"Me? So *I'm* responsible?"

Had he just accused her or defended his actions? Whichever, he couldn't take it back. She closed her eyes and sighed. The long one where he was totally on her bad side until something else happened to change her attitude.

"Come on, Kate. You know I'm talking about right here, right now, this particular situation."

"Really? Would it have happened at all if you'd been able to walk away from the Serna investigation when the threats began?"

"We don't have time for this." He pulled the saddle cinch, wanting to be eye level for where the next words would take them. He knew what was coming. What should have come a long time ago. She'd never accused him. Never yelled at him. Never told him he was responsible.

"You've never chosen to discuss it. That's why I divorced you." She turned her back to him, clicking to Candy to start moving.

"Right."

How many times over the past three years had he heard the words *if you'll just talk to me.* About what? They both knew what had happened when he'd gotten shot and, more important, when she'd lost the baby. Bottom line? He'd paid the ultimate price for not being there to protect her—he'd lost his family.

Talking about it wouldn't make it any better. He'd never understood why she thought it would. What more was there to say?

"Yeah, fall into that same old habit, Cord. Lock down and don't say another word to me. It's a long way to Nick's place. Good thing you decided a long time ago talking is one thing we can live without."

She heeled her horse, not waiting for him to mount, not heeding the potential danger still out there waiting. And not before he heard her mumble, "Thanks for the reminder."

He stepped into the stirrup and took off down the trail after his wife—ex-wife—began the all-day trek to her closest neighbor and high school sweetheart.

"Dammit."

Chapter Seven

"Do you see that, Cord?" Kate stretched tall in the saddle but couldn't see who was coming toward them.

They'd been riding the fence separating the Danver and Burke ranches for at least an hour. Cord had wanted to just cut through, but she'd refused. He'd given in when she reminded him that it was faster to get to the next cattle guard and follow the road. That had been the only conversation. They'd been in a hurry with a storm moving in and had taken very few breaks for the exhausted horses.

"Do you think it's Burke?"

She leaned forward, patting Candy's neck. "Can't tell. They're on the road from his place."

"It's unlikely Serna would send his men that direction. Logical to assume Sheriff Barber asked if we'd shown up there."

"If you say so."

Cord took the lead the last hundred yards to the gate. It didn't pass her notice that he'd brought the empty machine gun pistol around from his back for show. Or that he pulled the pistol from his waist. He rode Ginger with one hand on the reins and looked like a weathered cowboy in her dad's old coat.

The sorrow at taking a human life hit her chest right along with the fright of who was in that vehicle. Her mouth went drier than it already had been. She stuffed her gloves into her jacket and pulled her rifle to lay it across her lap. The apprehension made her belly turn over a couple of times, just like the first days of morning sickness.

Cord slowed to a standstill, waiting for the car to top the next rise. He didn't give any indication of what to do. Typical Cord. But he didn't have to. Candy whinnied at the tense hold of her reins. Kate tightened her thighs around her horse, who was ready to bolt.

"The dust is still flying so they haven't stopped. That's good. They had to have seen us. Stay alert, Kate. Tell me if you don't recognize someone."

Cord's voice had a dangerous, low warning tone, easily recognized from all the trouble they'd experienced together. She was glad for it, at least as much as she could be while waiting to see who would top that hill—gang member or close friend.

"That's Nick's Jeep."

"Yeah."

"Mr. Cauldwell's driving." Every muscle in her body melted. She relaxed Candy's harness and they ambled forward in line with Ginger.

Cord pocketed the pistol and grabbed her thigh. "Don't talk about it. Not a word to Nick, his foreman or anyone else. It's important. We can't trust anyone yet."

"Don't be ridiculous. You know Nick and Mac Cauldwell. They wouldn't hurt me."

"I don't know anything."

That cold steel edge in his voice pierced her heart, sending a shiver up her spine. He meant it and she should remember. *Don't trust anyone.*

"What about the drugs? Are you calling the Ranger headquarters or DEA or whoever you were working with? If they know about the cabin and the canyon, can't they arrest Serna? Wouldn't we be safer then?"

"I'll take care of the phone calls. Just don't give details to anyone. Period."

"Kate! Thank God!" Nick jumped from the doorless Wrangler and opened the gate for the horses. "We've had teams out looking for you since early this morning. It's lucky we found you, there's a bad storm moving in, shutting everything down. Some flash flooding is expected."

They dismounted while Nick was talking. Cord gave her strange looks when Nick hugged her.

"Where have you two been?" Mr. Cauldwell asked, his arm casually draped over the steering wheel.

"We didn't see anyone. Some rocks blocked the trail to the lodge so we trekked over here. Got a way to recall those searchers?" Cord sounded cordial enough from his horse's side, but Kate could feel the tension zinging from his actions.

The machine gun was gone from around his chest. When had he—and where had he—hidden it?

"We're dog tired, Nick. Got room in that thing for our gear?" she asked. She didn't want to be rude, but Cord had said not to talk about the details. "We've been riding on these dang horses much too long, I'm afraid. Hey, Mr. Cauldwell, I see you've taken up a much cushier ride."

She received the chuckle she'd hoped for from the older foreman, who didn't ask for more details. There was no one in Jeff Davis County that was faster throwing a rope around a steer. She'd known the man her entire life. Things wouldn't be the same when he retired.

"Here, let me help," Nick said as she lifted her leg over the saddle.

Before she could say no, he'd slipped his hands around her waist to help her down. As if she'd ever needed help.

Turning to face him and be polite with a thanks, she caught his expression of disillusionment. She'd completely forgotten no one outside the family knew she was pregnant.

"How's your dad doing, Nick?" She tried to act normal and hoped he wouldn't cause a scene.

"Always thinking about others. He's holding his own, Kate. In fact, he almost got dressed to come search for you himself." Nick's words were nice, but his questioning look toward her belly confirmed that he'd felt the baby. "So you guys are back together. You sit, I'll get your saddle. Mac will send someone for the horses when we get back."

Cord darted a look and a shake of his head, reminding her not to impart information. There weren't answers anyway. They were forever together in a sense. Whatever happened, they'd both be involved with the upbringing of their child. Not if Cord had his way and she disappeared into a witness-protection program.

Leaving her family? Her friends? Her heritage? Could she do that?

Suddenly very tired, all she wanted was a hot, soaking bath to ease the ache in her muscles. And just a few minutes forgetting what might happen to the rest of her life. A little peace after a phone call to her dad. *Oh, no.*

"Does my dad think we're missing?"

"You can use my cell as soon as we hit coverage," Nick said, stowing her stuff. "No one mentioned him, though."

"What exactly have you heard, Nick?" Cord asked, joining him with the saddle from Ginger. "How about you, Mac?"

Mac shrugged. "Nothing much. I do what I'm told these days."

"The sheriff called, said you'd gone missing in the mountains and taken Katie with you."

She hated being called Katie. It was such a sissy name.

She'd given Nick more than one bloody nose before they were in their teens for using it.

"I'll borrow your cell now."

Nick joined her, handed her the phone and leaned closer. "I'm going to assume this has something to do with Jorje Serna's release and that McCrea doesn't want you to talk to me. But if you need anything, and I mean *anything,* including getting away from your ex…I'm there for you."

Why did the offer send more *heebie-jeebies* up her spine?

AS HE WATCHED Kate's high school best friend and prom date lean in, essentially trapping her to the side of the Wrangler, his fists clenched. And not from the normal pain in his backside. He fought the urge to grab Burke by his coat collar and connect his knuckles with that artificially tanned face. But he was more than a little tired and would end up losing. If you're going to fight for a woman, you at least need to win the battle and look good. Right?

Kate had made it very plain he wouldn't win the war no matter what kind of shape he was in. He clenched his fists and shoved them in his pockets. Drawing on every Ranger discipline he knew—and a few shrink techniques— he cloaked his anger with blandness.

Kate shot him a questioning look as Burke put her in the front seat.

"I think I'll drive back to the house, Mac," Burke said.

Mac Cauldwell rolled his stiff old body from the Wrangler, popped the seat forward and crooked himself in back without a word. Unfortunately, Cord felt as old as the foreman he sat next to looked.

Burke stuck to the trek everyone referred to as a road, hitting every hole and rut along the way. Cord's back cramped more with each one the Jeep found. At least on the horse he'd been able to stand in the stirrups and relieve the pressure.

By the time they reached the main house, Nick had jabbered about the thunderstorm warnings and given them a play-by-play on the search for both them and Serna.

The gang leader should have been arrested before he left the courtroom. The lack of preparedness on the DoJ's part just confirmed that Serna had someone on the inside. He was missing something obvious. Had to be.

He'd been over the case files a hundred times. More than a hundred if the truth were told. Lord knows he had the time. Kate assumed he was back on the job, but he'd only been allowed back in uniform for court. There wasn't a desk for him in Valentine, Texas. Only desk work in Lubbock or El Paso. He wasn't ready to move and give up the daily reminder of what life could have been like before Serna had destroyed it.

Searching the case file for something he'd missed had become his routine while sitting in their empty house waiting. Waiting to leave for therapy—mental or physical. That was a fairly accurate description of his life.

Sleep avoided him most nights. Or he avoided sleep.

Dreams plagued him.

If the darkness wasn't filled with demons from the shooting, they were filled with thoughts of angels holding their little girl.

His thumb wrapped around his fingers again. The fists rested in his lap. They passed the cattle guard, pulling around to a row of cars and trucks to park. Mac patted him on the shoulder. When Cord caught his knowing look, the embarrassment made him physically relax his body but didn't help with the jealousy he tasted.

"I'm going to call my dad now," Kate said, jumping from the Jeep as if she'd been on a picnic instead of twenty-four hours of pure stress.

Cord recognized that tone in her voice. Burke had made two mistakes. One—she hated being called Katie. She'd told him that her father had chuckled when her brother had teased her with it while they'd grown up. Probably still did.

And the second was assuming that he'd told Kate to do anything.

Yeah, he could count on Burke getting a cold shoulder for the next couple of hours. It wouldn't be long afterward that they'd be gone. Of course, he didn't plan on letting Kate out of his sight very long.

But Kate didn't need to know their time schedule. Not yet.

"Dad? Yes, we're fine. What did they tell you?" Kate didn't head to the house. She took off toward Mrs. Burke's garden, her rifle in hand.

Nothing much there this time of year except privacy.

He threw his saddlebags over his shoulder and followed at a distance. Far enough away to not hear their conversation. Close enough to tell when she'd finished up.

"He wants to talk with you."

He took the cell and Kate walked to the kitchen door. He hadn't spoken to any member of the Danver family since before the divorce and had no idea what to expect during this conversation.

"Hello, David. Before you waste time complaining about the danger I've put your daughter in, understand that nothing will happen to her under my protection."

"Right now, Cord, you're the only one she trusts. Just get her to the airport tomorrow. They're telling us there will only be a short window between these merging storm fronts. We'll call as soon as we're allowed to lift off."

"That's not what I have planned, sir."

Silence.

Cord looked at the phone to make sure they hadn't been disconnected. "I don't believe it's safe to wait."

"I see. You think he's coming after you?"

"The less details I share with you, sir, the less danger your family's in." It wasn't that Cord didn't trust Kate's father. He just didn't know how thoroughly Serna's men had infiltrated the local area.

"You'll notify me?"

"Yes, sir." Cord had a few other things to say to convince David he was right. He hadn't planned on one hundred percent cooperation. Made for a shorter call.

"I'll tell your parents you're both all right and that you'll call when you can."

What an ungrateful son. He hadn't even thought about calling his parents to let them know he or Kate were okay. The Rangers had probably contacted his dad as soon as Serna was freed.

"Thank you for that." He paused. "And for your trust."

"Goes without sayin'."

The old man had thrown him off his rehearsed dialogue. He would never have thought David would openly support his decisions. "Wish there were more time to bring you up to speed, but—"

"Yeah, Kate told me a bit about the cabin and confrontation this morning."

"She didn't hesitate."

"That's what's bothering her, son."

"Sir? I..." Cord knew he needed to say the words. There was a chance he'd never see David Danver again. He owed him an apology. The shrink had stressed that ignoring everyone in his life for the past three years had hurt them. He knew that without the shrink's constant discussion. "I wanted to tell you—"

"This isn't the time for regrets, son. I would have kicked your ass a couple of times already if Kathleen hadn't stopped me. Take care of my little girl."

This time there was a distinct click as David Sr. hung

up. Cord dialed his parents' house phone. They should hear from him directly. His mom was probably worried sick. The call went straight to voice mail.

"Hey, Mom. Just wanted you to know we're okay and I'll be keeping Kate safe for a while. I'll call as soon as I can. Just borrowed this phone so there's no reason to call back."

He had a few more phone calls to make. He stuck the phone in the bag still hanging on his shoulder. Man, he was tired and starving and filthy.

Time to face Durke's mom and crew, get cleaned up and maybe—just maybe—give his aching back a rest. Their host was right about one thing. The storm moving in would complicate everything he had planned.

NICK'S MOTHER WAS a sight for very tired eyes. Juliet waved her inside through the back door.

"Oh, my dear, don't take this the wrong way, but you look awful." She pulled out a kitchen chair and gestured for Kate to sit.

"I probably do look a wreck." She removed the scarf and work coat and collapsed on the seat cushion.

"You sit down here at the table." Juliet tied her apron and paused. "Want coffee or hot chocolate?"

"Your famous chocolate, please."

"My grandmother said everything could be fixed with a good cup of cocoa and, after living so many years in this desolate backcountry, I tend to agree with her. Of course, I make Alan a cup every afternoon." She removed milk from the fridge and turned to the stove. "Not instant, mind you. I hate instant. Don't you? Well, even if you preferred it, I'd have to make it on the stove because I don't have any. Instant, that is. I don't like it so I don't buy it."

"How is Mr. Burke?"

"Staying busy. A rancher's work is never done. He rests

a lot, though. Takes things slower." Juliet wiped the corner of her eye with the back of her hand as she gathered more chocolate ingredients.

Tears? So maybe the rumor she'd heard about his remission was true and he wasn't doing well at all. How terrible for Juliet and Nick.

Hearing Juliet's voice reminded her how much she missed her father being around the house. This was exactly how he talked when he made his enchiladas. The one dish he excelled at and had perfected. He explained everything he did, each and every time.

Then it was her turn to cook and he'd chatted instructions nonstop until the pan was in the oven and the cheese bubbled to perfection. She'd asked him why when she was about seventeen. Being a smart-assed teenager, she'd patiently explained to him that she'd heard the recitation once a month her entire life and could repeat it by heart.

Of course, the next batch was the most horrible enchiladas they'd ever eaten because she'd had to prepare them on her own. After that, they cooked enchiladas together with her father talking her through every family secret along the way.

"Kate?" Cord was seated at the table with her. He nodded toward Juliet.

"Hmm?" She'd been so lost in thought, or so dang tired, she hadn't heard him come in the door.

"Toast or biscuits?" Juliet asked, looking concerned. "Are you too tired to eat, dear?"

"Oh, sorry. No, I'm starving. Food first, please."

"Toast, Mrs. Burke."

"Then I'll have to make biscuits for dinner. Now that I put the thought of them in my head it's the only way to get them out."

"I'm going to check in with Mac's men. Find out if they

saw anything." Cord stood, scooting the chair across the wooden floor that was older than everyone in the room added together.

"You go right ahead, dear. I'll have everything ready to throw in the pan when you get back. I'm just going to fry up some venison sausage."

The uniform pants didn't fit him as snugly as they had three years ago. He'd lost weight and gained a lot of muscle even over the past five months. It had felt really good on that couch, backed against his chest. Having his warm breath caress the back of her neck had caused some additional tingling that had kept her awake long past him falling asleep.

Before the shooting, his occasional light snores would wake her and she would shake him to tell him to go back asleep. Last night, she couldn't close her eyes until he was relaxed and breathing deeply.

Kate didn't want to be rude, but watching her ex-husband walk to the bunkhouse comforted her and she really couldn't concentrate too much on what Juliet was saying. She listened to the stories, remembering how many times she'd sat at this same table.

"Do you remember the first time we met, dear?"

"Yes, ma'am. Mom brought me over after you bought the place from Mac. She was the self-appointed, one-woman welcoming committee to Valentine."

"That's right. She brought us her homemade bread. I was so impressed she showed me how to make it on the spot. Said she got tired of running to the store when your brother used all the bread to feed the baby chicks. Did she ever break him of that?"

"Not until he stopped feeding the chickens as one of his chores." She laughed at the memory. "Angering mom to get out of the chore may have been the only reason he used the bread. Davy still hates feeding chickens."

She wiped her hands on her ruffled apron and held them out to Kate. A serious look consumed her normally cheery face.

Kate held on to Juliet's strong embrace. "I miss her."

"I do, too. I only bring it up because I want you to know if you need anything or need to talk to anyone, I'm here." Juliet looked directly at her stomach. "When I was pregnant with Nick…well, I missed my mother more at that time than I normally did."

"So you know about the baby?" Kate hadn't removed her jacket, uncertain if she wanted to share her news with anyone. She shrugged out of the work coat and let Juliet hang it on the back door hook. But it was time to stop avoiding what people would say. Maybe it was because Cord knew now.

"David told me. I hope you don't mind." She set the toast and homemade jam on the table.

"Not really. It's not like it's a secret. Everyone will know soon enough." She caressed the swell that would soon make her barrel-size.

"I may have complained when we moved here about this being a desolate country, but it's become my home. All of our friends have become family. So if I can help, I want to be there for you. And for your mom."

Kate was touched. She'd been so isolated on the ranch. She hadn't really spoken much with her father since he'd gone to her brother's. She hadn't wanted to bother him with ranch details. And she especially hadn't wanted to hear the worry in his voice.

"I know this is butting in, but you don't have anyone to push their nose in your business." She smiled. "You should tell that man how you really feel."

"Cord? He knows."

"He doesn't. He's all confused and worried. It's as plain as the whiskers on his face."

"I'm not the one who has him turning in circles. It's Serna and not knowing. *That's* why he's so worried."

Juliet released her hand and picked up the corner of her apron to move the hot pan back to the burner. She began turning the bacon. "You can trust me on this Kathleen Danver McCrea, that man does not think you love him."

"But…I don't." *I can't.*

"I had my hope of you falling in love with Nick and I think for a little while, so did he. But those days have long passed. I never thought twice about it after Cord came into your life. You look at him, well, just like your daddy looked at your mama."

Chapter Eight

They were stuck at Nick's overnight but Kate wanted to be on her way. It was hard to sit still. Hard to relax when Serna and his men were out there waiting. The unknown had never appealed to her. She liked family. Loved working the ranch. And had discovered she loved running it even more.

One of the many reasons she'd refused to run away before Serna had been released. She couldn't run—with the exception of away from Cord. But that was different.

She wrapped herself in a towel reluctantly, leaving her extended soak. Clothes presented a problem, but Nick's mom had loaned her some pajamas and all Kate really wanted was to slide into the comfy queen-size bed, curl up and sleep until the thunderstorm was over. Then it would be safe to drive without the threat of falling rocks or flash floods.

She pulled the drawstring tight on the bottoms and heard a soft knock on her door that was already swinging open. Cord leaned in the doorway holding a blanket and pillow. Hat pushed back on his head, still dressed in his uniform, he hadn't cleaned up a bit since they'd arrived at Nick's ranch.

"What have you been doing?"

"Hate to ask this, Kate. I know you're tired. Can you let me use your shower for a couple of minutes?" Her ex-husband was already unbuttoning his shirt, assuming she'd say yes.

"And what was wrong with the main bath Mrs. Burke told you to use?"

"Didn't have time."

"Too many secret phone calls trying to get us out of here sooner?" She crossed her arms over her braless breasts that he kept glancing down at. "What's wrong with the hall shower?"

"Actually, I was sitting outside your door, waiting. Probably nothing wrong with that shower. Better if I'm here."

Had he become a delusional paranoid? "Really? You think someone's going to attack me in the guest bedroom?"

He shrugged his shoulders free of the drab beige color and tossed it on the back of the chair.

"Just stay awake five minutes. Then I'll take care of watching over things." His hands went to his belt buckle.

"Don't you do that, Cordell." She waved her hands. His eyes dropped to her breasts again. "Oh, go on. But hurry."

Cord laughed at her embarrassment heading to the bathroom. She hadn't heard him laugh in so long, turning a bright red was worth it. She checked the mirror just to verify that, yes, she had changed to a *sunburned palomino* as Cord had nicknamed her.

The shower spray came on. She grabbed a throw blanket to cover her shoulders and shut the bathroom door. *Just like old times.*

"Ouch." She shook her thumb where the dried cactus had lodged. It was irritating more than painful, something that had happened more than once in her youth. She could see the thorn just under the skin and she needed a needle or tweezers. Each time her thumb scraped something it brought her back to pulling the trigger....

She wanted the reminder gone.

Creeping like a thief, she opened the bath door. Cord had his back to her, and she could see the white suds from the soap still clinging to the gorgeous muscles. She didn't blame them for wanting to try. Ignoring the body on the other side of the curtain, she slowly pulled open the medicine cabinet. No luck. Then the drawer. Yea, pin cushion.

"You don't have to be so quiet. You aren't disturbing me." The water shut off. Cord shook his head and drew the curtain to one side. He pointed past her. "Want to hand me that towel? Or I could stand here and let you have a longer look-see."

"You...that was fast."

"Towel?"

"Oh, yeah, sorry."

Her *ex*-husband reached around her to grab the matching towel to the one wrapped around her hair.

What was wrong with her? She'd seen a naked Cord many, many times. Her nipples tightened as did many other places in her body. "I, um, needed a needle."

Wow, thank goodness he wrapped the lower half of his body. That just left the desire to sleuth off those beads of water from his shoulders and chest. If she didn't watch it, she'd be breathing hard soon. She was just tired. They both were.

"You done with this?" He tugged the towel from her hair and hung it around his neck, using the ends to absorb some of the drops. "What happened? Want me to take a look?"

Without waiting for permission, he brought her thumb closer to his sharp brown eyes. He didn't release her hand when she tugged.

"I can do it."

"I'm sure you can, but it would be easier and quicker if I helped. Then you could hit the hay faster." He took the needle from the cushion. "This is in there sort of deep. When did you get it?"

She didn't want to say it aloud. She'd killed a man.

"Humph."

He could tell. He'd always been able to read her, especially when something was wrong. If only he could talk through a problem as well as he could spot one.

"Ouch!" She jerked her thumb away from where he'd stabbed it.

"Don't be a baby. You know this is how you get a thorn free."

"It hurts."

"Of course it hurts. You have a piece of cactus stuck in your thumb." He swiped his hands on the towel hanging around his neck and adjusted it to cover most of the skin.

The sweet strawberry-patterned towel blocked her from seeing most of the muscles he'd developed in the five months they'd been apart. "You mashing and prodding won't help."

"Let me see it." He drew her hand closer to his eyes again. But he didn't look; he had them closed. He wrapped his lips around her thumb and sucked.

Oh, wow.

"Cord McCrea, stop that. What do you think you're doing?"

"Just softening up the skin so it won't hurt as much."

"It's plenty soft."

"Yeah, I remember."

"Cord, I'm—we can't—"

"I'm not." He teasingly smiled at her.

"Yes, you are." She jerked her hand to behind her back, protecting more than just her thumb from him. She didn't need much of an imagination to know what was going on under that towel at his hips. She'd experienced it and her muscle memory was playing havoc with her restraint. Her body was desperately ready to see if she remembered anything about sex.

He rolled the needle between his fingers and held out his left palm. "I promise to behave. Now give me your thumb."

Reluctantly, she placed her thumb in his care again. But she didn't know if she was reluctant because he might break his promise or that he might keep it.

Chapter Nine

"They're here."

With all the hands called in for the search and now back at the ranch, it was difficult to find a place to make a very private phone call.

"What do you mean? Where's 'here'?" Serna's voice showed his frustration.

"At the ranch. They're cleaning up."

Together. Same bedroom. Good. Serna's punishment will mean more if they're together. Divorced or not.

"How long? Did they say where they've been? My men haven't checked in from this morning."

Hadn't the man learned anything? McCrea was good. Too good. That's why he had to be taken out before he was reinstalled to the task force. Something that would have already been taken care of if it weren't for Serna's personal vendetta. The man should have been killed while he couldn't walk and defend himself.

"Knowing McCrea, you should send more men to the cabin. The others are probably dead." He pulled the phone away from his ear until the string of curses ceased, then continued, "We need that chopper. And he hasn't said anything about their activities."

"I want them dead."

"I know what you want and that's your problem. I've kept

my end of the bargain for over four years. I'm taking a big risk calling you with so many people around."

"Your end will come much sooner if you don't deliver them to me."

He bit his tongue instead of explaining why it was useless to threaten him. Serna would be gone along with everyone else.

"The storm's going to delay everything in the operation. You have time to get the chopper and get the McCreas before they leave."

He disconnected the line. The storm actually made his part to take down Serna, frame the Danvers and succeed much easier. Of course he'd deliver the McCreas. They'd ridden their horses right where he'd hoped.

Serna's men were lax and took too much for granted. The ones on the mountain were also probably dead.

Dance with the devil and all that.

"GOOD GRIEF, JUST be still and let me finish."

"Ow." She stuck the pad of her thumb in her mouth, her pink nail a slightly darker shade than her lips.

"There. All done. I see you're still having your nails done." Cord looked at her toes, perfectly manicured, just like her fingertips.

No matter how much she worked on the ranch, she didn't miss her appointment for a mani-pedi. It was almost a ritual for her. He'd teased but never asked her to stop, because he liked it.

"You always made fun of my nails."

He did like it. Liked that she took time for herself. She deserved it.

to tell her. That shrink voice nagged him. His sessions full of reasons he'd pushed people away. And every session ended with a question about Kate. The same question nagging him to answer right now.

He'd avoided thinking about why he hadn't contacted her since the divorce. Then during the last session his shrink had thrown out this thought-provoking moment: *You know you can't move forward until you face the past. And Kate is your past, Cord. If you expect change, you can't continue to walk through life. Letting her go is necessary and it's going to be painful.*

"What is it?" she asked. "You *do* think my nails are silly. Well, I don't care. When all's said and done, I still like to feel nice." She pushed at his chest, trying to move past him in the little bathroom.

His hands fell to her middle, holding her in place. "It's not that. I was thinking about something else. Kate, I— Holy cow, what was that?" His hand was on the side of her belly. "I thought we just ate. That was a heck of a stomach gurgle."

"Cord, I think that…that's the baby." She put her hand over his, shifting his touch more to the center. "There. Feel that."

Their eyes met and all he could manage was a nod. He'd just *thought* the baby was real before. The depth of emotion welling inside him was about to erupt like the volcano that formed the mountains around them. He couldn't label them or put words to them, but he knew they were there.

"Is that the first time she's moved?" he asked.

She. Daughter.

That eruption knocked the barricade he'd stashed his numb heart behind. He'd thought he'd hidden it deep under a cover of recovery. The tears welled in Kate's eyes, her lower lip rolled between her teeth and she swayed backward.

They'd shared something special, something only they could understand. And he'd screwed it up. Twisted it with a memory of pain.

Say it. Tell her you're sorry for being an insensitive jerk.

He could fall to his knees and beg for forgiveness. Or he could ignore another moment she seemed to be waiting for words he didn't have. How long had the minute lasted? Sixty seconds that time? Or three years of hurt?

The amazing woman sighed—a new one he didn't know. Then she squeezed his hands. Move on? It's okay? God, he wished he was better at this.

"It really is amazing. I'm glad you were here. Why do you think the baby's a...a girl?" She stumbled over *girl* but recovered. "My bet's on a boy. The McCreas always have a son to pass the Ranger badge to. Don't they?"

Was it wrong not to want a boy? There couldn't be a replacement, but he wanted that little baby girl. He wanted to rock her in the antique crib Kate had found. She'd talked the dealer in Fredericksburg to lower his price and had scraped every spare dollar they had together for the purchase. The yellow-and-brown baby comforter was still hanging on the side.

He clasped Kate's free hand, bringing it to his lips. "That was quite a wallop of a kick."

"Or just a flip. I think she's done now." She moved away from him. "We need some rest."

"Right. As soon as the storm passes, we gotta move." He stepped back, wanting to pull the woman carrying his child into his arms. He didn't know what to think or assume. Didn't know why feeling his child move made him want to make wild love to her. "You go lie down."

Kate walked away, not looking pregnant at all from behind. But he liked the pregnancy. It looked as good on her as the nail polish. Okay, not a perfect comparison for such a beautiful woman. He knew what the crazy thoughts fir-
through his mind meant. The same reason he couldn't
ass Kate with his shrink. The same reason he hadn't

accepted Kate's phone calls or texts or letters or heard her name without aching for the part of him that she'd completed.

She's not your wife anymore. She'd divorced him the morning after they'd made their baby. He knew that. He deserved that.

He caught himself from falling with a hand on the counter. His legs were tired, but it was the scar that ached like a deep, wrenching wound. No physical reason that it should. The doctor said there wasn't a reason for it. But there were three strong reasons: Shane, Sarah and a baby girl who never drew her first breath.

He'd almost forgotten to cover the scar when he'd left the shower. Hopefully, Kate hadn't noticed since he hadn't faced her straight on. He pressed his palm into the scar, trying to ease the hurt.

"Thanks for the hospitality, Juliet. I can do the laundry. Just point me in the right direction," Kate said from the other room.

He stood straight, surprised at Kate's voice. He looked at his red-rimmed eyes and turned on the cold water to splash his face.

"I won't hear of it," Mrs. Burke answered. "You both get some rest."

That's what happened when he let emotions get caught in a loop in his head. His training dropped to nil. He hadn't heard the door open. *Pull yourself together.* He sucked it up, stowed the distracting thoughts in an imaginary box and tucked the towel at his hips tighter.

Get Kate to safety. First priority. Only priority.

She was curled on top of the bed with a light blanket covering her. He wasn't looking forward to the small desk chair in the corner where he planned on spending the afternoon.

"You going to lie down in the other room?"

"Go to sleep," he directed. "I'm staying right here."

"In the chair?"

"Yeah. I don't want to leave you alone."

"Then come lie down."

"That's not a good idea." Just the thought of her spooning that pretty bottom into him got his blood flowing faster.

"Good or bad, I'll sleep sounder if you're next to me and you'll sleep better if your back is relaxed."

He lacked the ability to say no. As much as he wanted those emotions to stay under lock and key...they weren't. He was just too tired and sore. He needed the comfort of stretching out and relaxing if he were going to fulfill his promise.

But he wasn't lying there naked. He'd already visited Burke's bedroom and lifted some jeans and a T-shirt.

"What are you doing?" Kate asked on a gasp.

He turned around, stretching a leg into the stiff jeans. "Getting dressed."

She was leaning on one elbow. Her eyes were huge and her mouth a perfect O.

"You've seen all this before, babe."

Tears dropped to her checks. She was seriously crying. What the h...? He zipped the loose pants and rushed to sit on the edge of the bed.

"I didn't mean to upset you. I didn't think about getting dressed. I mean. I didn't think you'd get mad about it. I sort of didn't think about it at all."

"Shh. You didn't do anything. It's just that...I've never seen this." She caressed the bullet scar in his chest with the tip of her finger, then down and around his side, leaning behind him. "Or this."

"Man, I'm sorry." He tried to stand to get the shirt but held him where he was.

one besides the doctor and nurse had ever seen let touched his back since the shooting. Certain, methodical hands he handled without a second thought. Their praise at how well he'd healed always left him hollow. He didn't feel healed. Not by a long shot.

Whisper-soft strokes soothed him in a way he didn't know existed. Kate's fingers barely skimmed the puckered and stitched scars he had memorized in his mind. The places he couldn't physically feel were worse. The touch disappeared, reminding him of so many times he'd yearned for it.

Too emotionally raw to take any more, he jumped up and grabbed his shirt.

She didn't beg him to come back, just stretched her hand out in a gesture for him to return. And he did.

For the first time since his partner had been murdered, he needed to trust those around him to keep watch. He drew the drapes to darken the room more than the storm already had and tried not to bounce the bed too much as he lay down.

He put his arms under his head on the pillow and stared at the ceiling, careful not to touch Kate. But she had other ideas. She scooted that luscious bottom next to his hip.

A familiar hand touched his side, tugging, wanting him to do what he feared the most. *Snuggle.* He turned, meticulously keeping his hands to himself. Kate laced her fingers with his and placed his palm on the baby.

"I know it's not forever and I hope you'll forgive me for asking it of you. But right now, this minute," she whispered, "I want to dream of our family."

God help me, but I'm going to let you.

Chapter Ten

"Thanks for putting us up, Mr. Burke," Kate said when they entered the dining room. She could smell fresh bread every time the swinging door opened and someone brought another dish to the table.

Cord followed her. Everything was ready for six people. Ron was seated at the head of the table, buttering a famous homemade biscuit. She was so hungry it was like she hadn't eaten a huge plate of scrambled eggs and bacon before they'd cleaned up.

"I think Juliet and Nick had a little more say in the matter than I did, but you're welcome." Mr. Burke bit into the biscuit, so hot the butter oozed out and dripped onto the plate.

Ron Burke was a little younger than her dad and probably should lay off the butter considering he'd had a major heart attack the year before. Sometimes a wake-up call and sometimes not. He looked the same though, a tough old coot who had been a businessman before turning rancher.

Being here brought back a rush of memories. When her mother had been alive, the Burkes had gotten together with her parents every other week. They'd shared so many stories about ranch work not being what they'd expected. Laughing their missteps in taking over the ranch had been a pic. After her mother died, the dinners had grown dwindled down to not at all.

The sad part was that they'd bought this ranch from Mac, one of her dad's best friends. Mac had withdrawn after taking the job of foreman here, in charge of the land that had been in his family for several generations.

Standing at the door to the kitchen, Mac helped Mrs. Burke carry the rest of dinner to the table. Kate was glad to see him join them. There had been so many years where he'd been too embarrassed over losing the ranch to associate with any of the families in Valentine.

"Hey, Mac, glad you could brave the weather to come for dinner." She liked Mac, always had. "There isn't a better cowboy in the county, or the next, or the next."

"I think someone's probably passed me up by now. These old bones just ain't what they used to be."

"Never," she said faithfully, but didn't receive a crack of a smile from him.

Everyone joined Ron at the table. Nick had been silent in the corner, waiting with his arms crossed. He pulled out her chair, but Cord seated himself at her side. She didn't want to giggle, but it was sort of fun to have them competing for her time again. Mrs. Burke gave her a knowing smile and Mac just shook his head.

"You going to tell us what's going on?" Ron asked, loading his mouth with a bite of pork chop, his plate already laden with food.

Cord shrugged. "You know the basics. Jorje Serna vowed to kill Kate and then me. He was released yesterday and Kate needs to get to safety."

"Why didn't you head back to your place? I mean Danver's, or utilize the sheriff? Seems like that would have been faster than crossing the dang mountain," Ron stated. He didn't even look at them. "Took all the hands from their work to search for you."

"Dad, give it up," Nick insisted. "It wasn't like they could

do a lot with the threat of the storm anyway. We got everything ready yesterday."

"Aren't you curious?" Ron asked his son.

Mac and Juliet silently ate their dinner, either ignoring
or totally used to the father-son arguments.

"Cord's a Texas Ranger, sir," Kate explained, hating that
everyone thought they had a right to know, for some odd
reason. "He can't really talk about his investigations. It's
always been that way. So naturally, we shouldn't say what
we saw or what happened."

Did anyone else at the table notice her voice change?
Maybe Juliet, since she'd actually looked up. She sounded
so full of regret and sadness. If she wasn't careful, she'd remember everything that had happened this morning. She
wanted to forget. She could still feel the Remington's reverb against her shoulder. She rubbed it and was surprised
at how bruised she felt.

"Sorry, Ron. It's simple really," Cord said. "Coming here
seemed a safer option than returning to Kate's."

Her husband had never wanted to discuss his cases with
her. Had always thought it was too dangerous. Then they'd
been threatened. And threatened again. And ambushed. And
he'd still held back details. The thought should make her
angry—angrier—but she wasn't. She was proud that he'd
kept his oath to the Rangers. But the world had changed.
There wasn't honor among thieves and there were no bound-
aries on the casualties of war.

"The news said Frank Stewart was murdered." Nick put
his fork across his half-eaten plate. "That true? Someone
got the jump on Frank?"

"Shame about Frank. Now there was a good man. Your
daddy liked him a lot," Ron said, and added another bite of
gravy and biscuit to his mouth.

As good as she knew the food to be, it tasted like dry,

lifeless cardboard. *Oh, good Lord.* She was about to lose it. She tuned everyone at the table out. Concentrated on the fork. One bite. Just one.

Too many thoughts swimming in her head. Regrets or mistakes? Death. Killing. She bit her lip to stop. Took another bite of biscuit and thought she'd choke. Half a glass of water, Frank's name, a chuckle, the words "was such a good man." How could she get out of here?

Cord was relieved the conversation had turned reminiscent and the focus was off what had happened on the mountain. Curious how no one had asked if they'd run into trouble. Of course, Kate had sort of told them not to.

"Now that dinner's over, I for one would like to know what really happened out there. Why did you insist on talking to the sheriff alone, McCrea?" Nick Burke looked between Cord and Kate.

Spoke too soon. Kate stiffened beside him. Others might not see it, but he did. Her eyes were too shiny. Tears. She was about to cry. Had to be because of the pilot, the guy she'd killed. The events of the past two days were catching up with her. She couldn't do this to herself. He couldn't let her do this to herself.

"Thanks for a great dinner, Mrs. Burke," he said, pointedly ignoring the question about their activities. He pushed away from the table and tugged on Kate's chair.

"Now, Cord, if you don't start calling me Juliet, I'm going to get a complex."

Probably the most genuine person in the room, Burke's mother reminded him a lot of his own. He'd love to pick up the phone and tell her about the baby. Shoot, maybe she already knew. Shake it off, man. Get Kate out of here.

"I'll say it again, but I hope I can make gravy like that one day," Kate said, placing her napkin on her plate.

"Just come over a couple of more times and Mom can give you lessons," Nick spouted, covering Kate's hand and squeezing.

She's your ex, and can leave her hand wherever she wants. Get over it.

"A lesson would be nice. Maybe after all this is over and done with I'll have some time."

Kate looked up at only him, expressing a pleading look of "save me." Was it his wishful thinking that she didn't want her hand under Burke's? Or just didn't want to make small talk about gravy lessons? Either way, the strain and tears were still in her eyes. Time to go.

"Sorry again to impose on you like this, but it's much appreciated. I'm done in. How 'bout you, Kate?"

"I hardly slept last night. I think I'll say good night." She finally stood and joined him.

Cord had his hand on her lower back, guiding her to walk into the hall first when Burke reached out. The sturdy control on his forearm wasn't a casual stop. Neither was the look from Kate's former beau.

"Mom said the guest room's ready."

"Not necessary since I'm not leaving Kate's side."

"Listen, McCrea." Burke stood, facing him toe-to-toe, dropping his voice to a threatening whisper. "Next time you want some pants, just ask."

Cord replied with a raised eyebrow. Let Burke interpret it any way he wanted. Kate was waiting in the doorway. Cord turned back to Mrs. Burke, pulling free from her son's grip. "If it's okay with you, Juliet, I might just have seconds on those biscuits and gravy later."

"That's fine, dear. Just fine. Glad you like 'em."

When he looked back at Kate, it wasn't the threat of tears he saw in her eyes. Nope, that long sigh and the slight shake of her head meant she was disappointed. Again or always.

He closed the bedroom door behind them and turned the lock. Not real protection, but it would have to do. Kate's hands were balled and planted on her hips. He knew the routine and it wasn't something he wanted at the moment. Arguing about his behavior would just avoid what she needed. Yeah, that pattern was something he'd become an authority on in the past three years. He'd mastered the process to perfection.

"You didn't ask for his jeans?"

"No."

"Your mother would be so embarrassed. *I'm* embarrassed."

"Well, don't be." He shrugged out of the button-up he'd been given to wear to dinner. "As you're constantly reminding me, we're not married anymore."

"Get out. Go sleep in your own room. I'm perfectly safe here."

"We need to talk, Kathleen."

"Right. You mean, you have instructions to give and I need to listen."

"I know you're upset."

"You bet your patootie, I'm upset. The Burkes have been nothing but gracious to us and you stole Nick's jeans."

"You shot a man."

"Oh." She swiped a pillow off the bed and sat in the desk chair, wrapping her arms around the softness and hugging herself. Visibly deflated and dejected, her shoulders dropped. The fire left her eyes and yet they sparkled as they filled with tears. "What's going to happen?"

"Is that what you're really worried about?"

He waited. If there was one thing he'd learned after a year of therapy, it was that whoever was asking the questions waited until they were answered. You couldn't rush the conversation.

"No."

"It couldn't be avoided."

"I still killed a man," she whispered.

He hooked her hair over her ear to see her face more clearly. "Does it scare you more that you *shot* a man or that you don't regret it?"

"I regret it! I do." Her head jerked up, but her face wasn't full of indignation, it was full of questions.

"There's probably truth in that and there should be. What you have to hold on to and remember is that he would have killed me. And he would definitely have killed you." He gently moved the pillow to smooth her shirt over her belly. "Snuffing out two heartbeats with one shot if he'd had the opportunity."

"I know all that." She tapped her temple. "But how do you live with it every day? You never talked about this part of your job."

"I guess I never did. If I'd ever had to shoot someone, maybe I would have. I don't know."

"Wait. You never—before that night—?"

"Nope. And I don't remember shooting Serna's brother. The first guys that I can remember happened this morning. And you're right. There's a touch of regret for the loss of life, but I'm right. We didn't have a choice. They would have killed us or taken us to Serna, who would have done worse."

There were worse things than dying. Watching someone you love suffer or, worse still, be tortured. Surely that was worse than losing your life? He never wanted to find out.

"Thing is, babe…" He took a knee next to the chair so he could see her downcast eyes. "I wouldn't hesitate to protect you again. Not a second. Let another bastard try."

She tossed the pillow to the floor and wrapped her arms around his neck. He felt the hot tears on his skin. Man, she smelled good. Holding her felt good. Didn't matter why he was holding her. She belonged in his arms. He let her cry and when she was exhausted and the hiccups began, he lifted her, keeping her tucked close, and took her to bed.

As much as he ached for her, she was no longer his, and holding her would have to do. But they'd traveled through an impasse of his making. Maybe the shrink was right. Maybe they could talk through that night and what happened after. It wasn't something he looked forward to, but maybe, just maybe, they'd taken the first step on the journey back to each other.

Chapter Eleven

They were up from a second nap, rested and hungry again. The storm was letting up and it was pitch-black outside. As soon as Cord could, they'd snatch a set of keys from the rack and borrow a car. When they reached Kent, he'd "borrow" another one. His only plan at the moment was to keep them moving so Serna couldn't find them.

"I thought we were getting dressed for a midnight snack? Why are you packing?" Kate asked.

"I don't think it's a good idea to hang around." He hedged, since he hadn't told Kate her family wouldn't be at the airport. The subject would come up soon enough and the thought of flying tomorrow seemed to ease the tension for Kate. If Serna knew no one could fly in, it also meant that they couldn't use any airstrips to escape. So he'd be watching the roads even closer.

"Sorry, but we're here for a while. The weather front is not cooperating with your timetable, Cord. A front in Colorado is headed this way with possibly additional fronts pushing into the area from the west late tomorrow. Dad said they couldn't fly until after the snow. It's okay to wait here and be safe."

Not okay with him. As for being safe? Well, the Ranger task force were certain Serna had an inside man at most, if not all, the ranches in this area. It was one explanation why they'd been using the mountains so openly. And success-fully. No matter how much hospitality the Burkes showed them, he didn't trust Nick.

He had to obtain the right vehicle and drive her some-where safe. As soon as he figured out where that could be. He'd confirmed a time to call David. If he didn't, it meant they were in trouble. Kate's father was the only person he trusted beside himself to keep her safe. The man didn't need much explanation or convincing. He'd been begging her to get out of Texas for weeks.

If anything went wrong, Cord was solely responsible.

Her father agreed that Cord should get her out as soon as physically possible. They couldn't wait patiently for po-lice protection, at the ranch or at a secret location. There was no secret location. Not where Serna was concerned. And they couldn't hang around the airport waiting on the chance the weather would clear before Serna found them to take his revenge.

"The longer you stay here, the more danger you're in, Kate."

She walked from the bath where she'd been dressing, holding a large Texas Tech sweatshirt—Burke's. "Why do you hate Nick?"

"I don't hate Burke." He intensely disliked the man.

"You don't like him," she clarified.

"He doesn't really care for me, either."

"You think he's attracted to me? Still?" She laughed, pointing to the swell in her stomach, very apparent again under the thermal shirt.

"Darn certain he is." He sounded just like the jealous husband. Damn. He was the jealous ex-husband.

If Kate had attended Tech in Lubbock instead of UT in Austin, their paths would never have crossed. They'd never have met and he wouldn't have taken this assignment to stay in the area. She'd be the younger Mrs. Burke by now. She wouldn't be in danger. And she wouldn't look at him with those disappointed sighs gracing her luscious lips.

"You shouldn't dislike him because we were good friends growing up."

"That's not the reason. Let's drop it." *The man's still in love with you, Kate. Can't you tell?* Tell her. Say it out loud. Tell her how you've missed her, how your arms ache to hold her every night.

"Right. Nothing's changed," she said.

No, nothing about his feelings had changed. He pulled on his boots, wishing he'd had something with thicker, sturdier soles for climbing earlier in the canyon.

"What's going to happen to us here?" she asked with her fingers paused on the doorknob.

"Put on your boots."

"Really? I wanted to keep my toes near the fire and get some more hot chocolate and biscuits."

"We need to be ready to move. I don't trust—"

"Anyone."

"Now's not the time to explain."

In spite of the disgust he heard in her voice, she grabbed her shoes and sat in the chair to tie them. He'd protect his family no matter what she thought about his *trust* issues.

"Set the phones on the table, will you?"

"We can't take them?" she asked, standing near the end of the bed, dragging a finger across the rifle barrel currently wrapped in a towel. "Where did you get the backpack?"

"I kept the SD cards." He gestured to the pack. "Mrs. Burke thought it would be easier to carry our stuff. I left the saddlebags with our tack."

"She didn't see the machine gun, did she?"

"Nope. Not unless you showed her."

"Right. Are those boxes of cartridges? Nick gave you—"

He stiffened at the word "gave," giving himself away.

Realization spread across her face. "Good grief, Cord. You broke into his gun cabinet?"

"He should have better security. Too easy. I used a pocketknife."

"I cannot believe you'd do such a thing."

He stopped her from pulling the door open. Then stopped her from talking by slipping his hand over her lips. "You made me promise. I gave my word to protect you and the baby. Do you honestly think we're safe here?"

She shook her head and he dropped his hand. The fear of what Serna would do to her shook his core. He blocked it from his mind. If he got emotional, he'd lose focus. He needed to focus. Have a plan and a backup plan and a backup plan to that.

"Is this going to end, Cord?"

The words were on the tip of his tongue to tell her everything would be okay. Things would change. They'd be fine. He wanted to lie. He couldn't. Not to Kate.

Her arms wrapped around his neck, pulling him to her in a moment of frightened clarity. When she looked up at him, tears pooled in eyes that never deserved to cry but had too often. He bent closer and captured her lips.

Five months, five days without feeling the surge of power he'd always experienced with her kiss. A strengthening power that recharged his entire being. Knowing that she was the only person who'd ever made him feel…anything. The knowledge floored him. Knocked his feet out from under him when he realized he may never feel that again. She kept him from losing control.

No one except Kate had been able to catch him in a free fall. She'd been the only woman he'd wanted since they met.

The natural hunger from her startled him. His brain screamed at him. Go further. Take more. You want her and, more important, you need her. Her body melted into him. Why had he wasted the past several hours on sleep?

Their tongues tangled, desperate for each other. Logically, it wasn't a good idea, but with Kate in his arms he couldn't behave logically. He just wasn't that strong. Only his body was reacting. And right then, the loose jeans he'd borrowed were getting pretty dang tight.

Man, he needed her. He cupped each side of her face and devoured her lips. Every aching, hungry attack was countered with her own. Her hands were on his chest, raising his shirt, skimming along his rib cage. When he hesitated, her mouth sought his. They collided together, twisting closer. The back of his knees hit the edge of the bed.

"I can't..." She stopped, pushing back. "We can't go there. This can't happen. I'm sorry."

Cord released her as if she were a hot branding iron. He commanded his body to relax. Almost. He shoved the second box of ammo into the pack along with water and food he'd taken when Mrs. Burke wasn't looking.

"Cord..." Kate wrapped her fingers around his shoulder and he jerked away.

"Don't. I get it. We're divorced."

"I don't want to hurt you."

He stood straight, threw the strap over his shoulder and forced his voice not to shake. "We're past that."

You can't hurt someone who's already dead inside.

Kate followed Cord from the bedroom, where they'd spent a few peaceful hours. The storm had taken a south turn toward Marfa and was easing up a bit. The brief hail that accompanied it had awoken her from a sound sleep before dinner. One of two she'd had safely wrapped in Cord's arms.

It brought memories of happier times before the shooting, but not as much as the kiss. Oh man, to be kissed like that every day again. Cord was such a good kisser.

And such a good lover. She missed him so much, but she couldn't go back. It was impossible not to wonder if she'd ever feel safe without him. Shoot, it was impossible to be with him and wonder if she'd ever feel safe. Now she had another life to think about.

It was so sad to admit they were finished. Maybe if she weren't pregnant she would give him a second chance. Perhaps. But the baby changed everything. If Serna weren't the problem, some other gang Cord investigated would be.

Seven years ago, Cord's life had seemed exciting, adventurous. Now she knew it was just deadly. Being a Ranger was bred into Cord. It was a part of him, just like breathing was to a normal man. She placed her hand on their baby. Right now she needed lots of normal.

She wished with all her heart that they were secure, but as Cord continually reminded her, they weren't. Her strong Texas Ranger was prepared for an assault. And that's the reason she'd wanted his promise to protect her himself. He really was the only one she trusted to think of her first.

"Where is everybody?" Cord asked, leading the way to an empty TV room.

"Juliet mentioned they were heading to bed soon after we went to our room. It's after midnight, and this is a ranch with chores at the break of dawn. Most people are in bed. But speaking of dinner, I'm starved again. Leftovers are in the fridge."

He'd shut down and wasn't looking at her. Not ignoring, just not looking.

"Perfect. Leave it wrapped up and bring it with us."

"If you have some type of master plan, now would be a good time to fill me in on it."

He whipped her around, cupped her chin to meet his eyes, his jaw clenched tight in Ranger mode. "Trust me."

Two could play that stubborn game. She knocked his gentle grip away. "I do trust you, Cord. You are absolutely one of the few people I completely trust with my life. But don't take that as compliance and a reason not to keep me in the loop. We both know how *that* turned out this morning."

"I'm sorry, but we're leaving. Now." His voice was low and very determined.

"That's ridiculous. Dad can't get here until late tomorrow." She'd spoken to her father, had confirmed with Cord that they'd wait until the storm front cleared Colorado.

"Your dad's not coming. We're meeting him somewhere else. I spoke with him, too. He agreed it's too dangerous to wait."

Even trusting Cord's experience, she was not a child. The men in her life didn't get to arbitrarily make decisions for her. "You should have discussed this with me. I'm not asking why you didn't, but do you think you could disclose this mysterious location?"

"Dammit, Kate. We need to move. I'll explain on the road." He swung the pack over his shoulder, then grabbed all the key rings, sorting them into two hands.

"Are you serious? What are you doing?"

"No keys, no one can follow."

"These are the good guys, Cord. What if we need their help?"

"Grab the food and let's get out of here." Cord threw her jacket and Nick's sweatshirt at her.

"I need my cell phone."

"We're leaving them here. We can't risk being tracked that way."

Trust him, he knows what he's doing. She hurriedly pulled both on, not looking forward to the downpour of rain that was about to soak through all of it. In spite of her indicating he couldn't order her around, she'd go. She had to. She grabbed the plate wrapped in foil and the extra biscuits from the stove left in a ziplock.

"Can you tell me where we're going and at least grab a car with a heater?"

The next couple of minutes were a blur. Between the rain and Cord being her human Kevlar, she didn't see much. She watched the ground where she was running, trusting that he could see the rest of the yard and bunkhouse where the men could be. He dropped all the keys inside a car once he found a Wrangler with four-wheel drive.

They left like thieves without anyone running down the drive after them.

"Before you get all curious again asking a ton of questions, help me watch the road. Will ya?"

He laughed when she acknowledged him with a low growl of her own. The man was so very frustrating. She waited. Not patiently. She cranked the heat up, tapped her wet shoes on the floorboard, removed her jacket and stared at the barely visible wet gravel.

If her behavior annoyed him, he didn't show it. When she glanced in his direction he had a smile on his face. A very frustrating man.

"North. Definitely not the shortest route to civilization," she stated when he turned onto the main road.

"Nope, but it's the shortest to Interstate Ten and New Mexico. Rain's letting up."

"Can I eat now? I know you can't, but I'm starving." She didn't wait for approval, glad that the pork chop was something she could hand him later to eat on his own. "Juliet was nice to make us homemade biscuits. I haven't had peppered gravy like that since high school."

"Trying to torture me with talk of food? I snuck an extra one when I grabbed the water. Got some of that gravy, too."

Frustrating. Now all she could think about was thick peppered gravy. The exact type her mother excelled at and she couldn't personally ever get right. What she wouldn't give for her mother to be here when the baby came.

No tears. Anything could be on the road now. She needed to see and shouldn't get all emotional. *Just eat and watch.*

Living in the mountains, you got used to traveling cautiously around curves and inclines. There were enough of both to slow you to a snail's pace with even a smidgen of bad weather. Cord was a great driver and wisely braked at the right places.

A lot of time had passed, but they hadn't driven far in the rain, looking for fallen rocks and debris. Kate had been watching carefully but was scared witless when Cord brought the Jeep to a skidding halt on a desolate stretch of road.

"Should I ask what you see that I don't?"

"Backup lights around the next curve."

"Someone's waiting for us? How did they know?" She saw his raised eyebrow with the glow of the dash lights until he pushed the button cutting everything off. "This doesn't mean anything, Cord. Nick's place is the closest around. They must have been watching. No one there called Serna's men."

"Right."

It wasn't the time to tell him his I'm-a-Texas-Ranger-and-know-everything attitude didn't help their relationship. Or get a cooperative attitude. So it was up to her to just ignore it. She could do that.

"How do we get around them?"

"We can't."

"Then we turn around? Just tell me what your plan is. Good grief, Cord, you are so frustrating."

"We walk," he said, backing the Jeep to the side of the road.

"You think they've got someone waiting on the south road, too." Leaving the car was insane. How could he possibly think they'd be successful? What were the odds they could be? "You're serious that we should walk?"

"You know I am."

She did know and didn't argue. "It's going to be a tremendously hard hike. Cold, muddy…it may continue to storm, maybe snow. We have no camping or climbing gear. Shoot, we don't even have raincoats. And you want us to hike straight over a mountain—in the dark?"

"Don't forget, Serna's men will probably follow us."

"Sounds like fun," she said with as much sarcasm as she could muster.

"Glad you agree."

If they headed west, they'd be completely in the open and easily seen in daylight. So east over the mountain was the only way. In normal weather and daylight, the hike might take them several hours. Probably an entire day. Under these conditions and without the proper supplies…

"Cord?"

His hand covered hers, stretched over their child. "I know. I won't let anything happen to you, babe. Either of you. But it's our only option."

She put on her outer coat, scarf and gloves, attempting to keep as much warmth for as long as she could. She popped the door open and Cord pulled her around to face him.

"I swear it, Kathleen."

The raw promise in his eyes gave her the confidence to take the first step on a hellish journey.

Chapter Twelve

What the hell had he been thinking? When he watched Kate's feet slip on loose rocks, his heart paused, taking a full second to catch up with the realization that she hadn't fallen. Ten or fifteen minutes and the stress began taking its toll. He could only imagine what this hike would do to Kate. They couldn't afford to stop and discuss how the near misses were affecting her.

Near misses? This was nothing. This was a path at the bottom of the hill that was at the bottom of a steep grade to the top. To avoid the steep rock faces, they'd have to walk a couple of miles either direction.

Kate stopped and began stretching her back. "Sure wish we had a flashlight." She waved her hand at him and caught her breath. "Oh, I know we couldn't use it now. They'd be able to see it from the Burke's ranch house. But I wish we had one for later."

"Do you think I should go first?" he asked, uncertain if it were safer to climb in front and check the path or behind her in case she fell.

She threw her gloved hands in the air. "I'm moving as fast as I can," she said, the frustration of talking to him plain in her voice.

"That's not why I asked."

"Oh. Well, I don't think there's a good—or safe—way to accomplish this, Cord."

He looked back to the Jeep as he had every two minutes. A car dome light flickered on and off. "They found the car."

"We should get moving. Any idea where we're heading? Especially without our cells?"

"We couldn't use them without being found, babe." The familiar endearment slipped out before he caught himself.

"There's nothing on the other side other than the state park and observatory."

"Then that's where we head. The observatory has satellites. People equal phones and they have a field for a helicopter to land."

"Good grief, do you know how far that is? What's wrong with hitching a ride to the highway?" She rolled her shoulders, swung her arms back and forth as if she were warming up for her workout video.

"Not safe. We don't know who's in the car—driving or holding a gun to the back of their head."

She shared a deflated long sigh. "You're right. I don't want anyone else hurt. But you know we're headed to the highest point in the mountains and there isn't *anything* between here and there. No ranches, no Ranger stations and we have no cell phones."

The heavy mist that would have eventually soaked them turned into bigger plops on their jackets. Kate got hit in the face. All she had was that old crocheted thing she'd made with her mother many years ago. When he'd "borrowed" his jeans and shirt, he should have found Kate a suitable brim to keep the rain off her.

"Better get after it then. Wait." He placed his favorite hat on top of her worn cap. She gave him a genuine smile with lots of white, straight teeth and didn't argue.

Kate set a steady, careful pace. Easy for him to follow

and keep watch for men who might be following. So far there weren't any lights flashing around below. Their mud-caked boots—neither pair made for hiking—contributed to the consistent slipping, adding another layer of danger to their journey.

Within minutes they were soaked. The temperature had to be just above freezing. Cord glanced at his watch again. They'd been climbing forty-five minutes with very limited headway. Kate slowed for another short catch-her-breath minute. They'd taken several and his back was more thankful than his lungs.

"There's too much rain to locate our position," he shared. "Think we should use a compass?"

Even at the slow pace she'd maintained, Kate huffed a couple of times before answering. "At this point, using a compass is pointless. There's really only one path—even though I use that term very loosely." She put her head down to avoid the pelting rain and took another step, falling to her knee, then waving him off. "I'm okay. Better get used to it. A scraped knee will soon be the least of our worries."

She pointed to the rock face just above them. This little trek wouldn't get them over that. They'd have to climb.

God help him, but how had things come to this? *He* was the one putting his wife in harm's way now. *Ex-wife.* The shrink's voice popped into his head. *She's forever tied to me now,* his own voice replied. Family. He could think of his child and his child's mother as family.

"We can't attempt to climb in this weather. I don't think anyone's following—they probably haven't been since they didn't know which direction we'd taken off."

"And this isn't the logical choice."

"Nope." He pointed ahead. "There enough trail to make it to the bottom? Might find a bit of an overhang for protection. If we stop here, we're fairly exposed to the elements."

"I can make it, Cord. Don't worry about me." She turned and got going.

From the looks of things, they had at least another hour and a half before hitting the base. He stretched his back, swung his arms a bit slower than Kate had. The pain shot up his spine with the first step.

"I know you can make it, superwoman," he mumbled to himself. "It's me I have doubts about."

"THE RANCH HANDS were told that the McCreas left the Jeep when they were picked up by the Sheriff's department." He leaned against the post in the bunkhouse, crossing his arms, looking—if not feeling—like he was unconcerned.

The hands had gone home when the rain let up. He'd lied as a couple passed the unattended Jeep, bringing attention to the missing couple. If it hadn't been for his warning, Serna's men would have been caught standing there with their thumbs tied to their automatic weapons.

"And they bought it?" Serna asked, demanded and shouted all on one long exhale.

The idiot had arrived shortly after the hands had left. He'd be lucky if no one in the main house noticed the lights out here. If they did, he'd explain it. He always did.

"Why wouldn't they? They don't suspect anything." He relaxed his face as soon as he realized he'd been scowling. He didn't appreciate being constantly questioned. It irritated the hell out of him, and it killed him to hold his tongue.

"We should send the men out to hunt them down like animals." Serna paced the length of the room like a caged mountain cat, a disgusted look on his haggard face as he passed each of the six men trying to dry off.

Serna's boys looked like drowned Chihuahuas. It took a lot of control not to laugh at their ruined expensive shoes. He covered his mouth with a hand, determined not to make a bad situation worse by taunting their stupidity with a smile. They were in the damn mountains dressed in slacks and imported footwear.

"Waste of time right now. Your men ain't experienced and you have no idea which direction McCrea took off. Best to just use the chopper."

Serna slapped the old pine table in the middle of the room with both palms. "We don't have another pilot here till morning. You said it would take another hour to get him to the canyon and then there are repairs."

"Yep, there is that."

Serna fingered the butt of his handgun while getting close enough that the stinking, stale smell of cigarettes drifted from his heavy breathing. "Be careful of your tone, my *friend*. Have you forgotten our deal?"

Such a jackass.

He stood straight, pushing himself closer. "I haven't."

A gun was pulled to his left. A loud warning to back off. The kid Serna had chastised that morning was just new enough to think he might be making a place for himself if he pulled the trigger. Drawing a deep, silent breath through his nose, he reminded himself of his endgame. The money. Serna was just a bad card necessary for the first round. But, unlike the unknown card he might be dealt, the winning pot was within his grasp.

He just needed to hold his tongue a little while longer.

"Can you remind your boy we're on the same side? Guns make me nervous." Far from it, there was a fully loaded peashooter in his inside jacket pocket.

"You're in the wrong line of work, friend."

"Edward, go sit with Ricky." Serna waved off the kid, who retreated. Then gestured to the table. "Come, sit. We'll relax."

"Radar said snow's likely. Just a suggestion, but you

NO POSTAGE
NECESSARY
IF MAILED
IN THE
UNITED STATES

BUSINESS REPLY MAIL
FIRST-CLASS MAIL   PERMIT NO. 717   BUFFALO, NY

POSTAGE WILL BE PAID BY ADDRESSEE

HARLEQUIN READER SERVICE
PO BOX 1867
BUFFALO NY 14240-9952

If offer card is missing write to: Harlequin Reader Service, P.O. Box 1867, Buffalo NY 14240-1867 or visit www.ReaderService.com

HI-L7-05/13

GET FREE BOOKS and FREE GIFTS WHEN YOU PLAY THE...

Lucky 7

Just scratch off the silver box with a coin. Then check below to see the gifts you get!

SLOT MACHINE GAME!

YES! I have scratched off the silver box. Please send me the 2 free Harlequin Intrigue® books and 2 free gifts for which I qualify. I understand I am under no obligation to purchase any books, as explained on the back of this card.

❏ I prefer the regular-print edition
182/382 HDL FV6W

❏ I prefer the larger-print edition
199/399 HDL FV6W

FIRST NAME

LAST NAME

ADDRESS

APT.#

CITY

STATE/PROV.

ZIP/POSTAL CODE

Worth TWO FREE BOOKS plus 2 FREE Mystery Gifts!

Worth TWO FREE BOOKS!

Worth ONE FREE BOOK!

TRY AGAIN!

Visit us at: www.ReaderService.com

HI-L7-05/13

might consider leaving while you can still get to that pilot of yours." He opened the door next to him.

"Always thinking. Nice." Serna's words didn't reflect the anger trapped in his eyes.

The man wants to kill me as badly as I want him out of the way.

But he left. And thanks to the storm, no one at the house heard their jacked-up cars start or leave. If they had, there would be lights and coffee. The others wouldn't hesitate to ask what was going on. There had already been too many questions about why McCrea had left without telling anyone.

Fortunately, it had been written off as part of the Ranger's overcautiousness concerning Kate.

Two days. That's all he needed. Just two days. If the weather cleared and held, he'd be free of this pompous jackass, the men with imported shoes and, most important, the distraction the McCreas were causing.

Chapter Thirteen

"This is good, Kate," Cord called from the first level spot they'd come to since they'd run out of path.

Kate could see a slight—very slight—jutting of rocks that might block a smidgen of the rain. She got another handhold, positioned her right foot and used what was left of her biceps. Her arms shook. The rest of her body felt like deadweight as she tugged and searched with the toe of her boot for the foothold she'd spied a few minutes earlier.

"I swear, Kate, this is as far as we go tonight," he demanded, his hands resting on his waist, legs spread to support him, and his serious face tipped up. "Promise me!"

She knew he was shouting. It was the only way to be heard between the cracks of thunder. The lightning didn't worry her. During one of the flashes, she could see that the cars next to Nick's Jeep were gone. Hopefully, so were the men.

But she was cold. Wet. Exhausted. And tired of the rain pelting her face. Or Cord's. Thank goodness Cord had been below her and caught his hat when it tipped and blew off her head.

With rock under her toe, she used her very sore thigh muscles to get a little closer to their perch for the rest of the night. One more and she could…

No more up. Her right hand connected with a flat surface—okay, flat compared to what they'd been looking at over the past hour. "Almost there."

"Please be careful. Slow."

If I moved any slower I'd be a slug. "Got it."

Left hand. Bring up your first foot. And now the second. Almost.

"Kate!"

Oh, God. No!

Her bare hands skidded across wet, slick rock as she desperately used all ten nails to grip anything. Nothing. Her left boot found a larger rock, stopping the downward slide. She'd fallen at least three feet. The three scariest feet of her life.

"Stay where you are!"

She couldn't do anything else. She'd barely heard him with the blood blasting its thump-thump-thump to prove she was still alive. It would take her a minute to get her racing heart under control so she could climb. Her hands were torn to shreds and she had no idea how to get them to work. She couldn't get her eyes to open.

It seemed safer to keep her focus on the backs of her eyelids.

How are you going to do this, Miss frozen-in-place?

There's a way. One hand. Let go and move one hand. Search for the next handhold. Kathleen McCrea, you have to think of the baby. Move it!

She couldn't. If she moved an inch…if she let go… The sensation of falling took over. She had to hold on. Just stay put until it was safer.

But the hard reality was she couldn't manage to stay there much longer.

"Cord? I…I'm not sure I—"

"Shut up, Kathleen. You have to do this. We're going up."

Kate knew she moved. Cord talked her through every

grip. It seemed that he watched every breath she took. And then they were at the ledge again.

"What now?" she asked, not certain it was loud enough to be heard but unable to maintain strength anywhere other than her fingers.

"Stay put. Don't move or talk or open your eyes. And especially don't argue with me."

He knew her too well.

And this once, she didn't object to being told what to do. She couldn't laugh about it. He was right. She had to concentrate on holding on. Staying put. Maybe after everything was over…

"Kathleen!"

"Yeah?"

"Give me your hand, hon."

Cord was above her, on the ledge. He had a death grip on her wrist. He pulled, and she braced her feet, helped as much as she could. He switched from her wrist and arms and tugged on her coat. Lying on her belly—halfway on the rock, halfway hanging—he grunted loudly and she shot onto the three-foot ledge.

Kate joined Cord's hat, placing her back to the wall, covering her face with her blood-scraped hands. Breathing deeply and crying loudly.

"You're safe, Kate. The baby's safe. We're all safe. It's not your fault," Cord whispered in her ear. "Come on now, hon. Look at me."

"My fault?" She did look at him and sat. Water streamed across his concerned forehead, running down the tip of his nose. "Why do you think I'd blame myself?"

He grinned crookedly, lifting the right side of his mouth and slightly shaking his head. He tossed his hands a bit into the air, turning to join her by resting against the rocks.

As uncomfortable as it was, she was tremendously grateful to be there.

"Oh, I know it's my fault. Everything usually is nowadays. *You* were the one saying it." He pulled his knees to his chest and obviously stretched his back.

"I didn't say…" Shoot, maybe while she was crying she had. It didn't matter. She was done with the pity party. "Do you think we'll be safe enough here to sleep?"

"That was the plan at the last ledge. You going to sleep this time?"

"Yes. You going to share your warmth?"

"Sure." He held up his arm and she slid into place. "I'll take my hat back unless you need it."

"No," she said, handing his hat to him and snuggling into the crook of his arm. "This is perfect."

And somehow…it was.

THE SUN RISING over the ridges to their left woke him, but as stiff as he was, he didn't move. He was stretched on his side, Kate wedged between him and the mountain, her arm stuck under his. Her hands were gloved once again and snug inside his jacket pocket.

They'd shifted to lying next to each other once the rain stopped.

"Good morning," she said.

"Morning." He attempted to sit up.

"Not yet. I finally got halfway not cold."

"Halfway not cold?" he asked, giving in since he wasn't ready to move, either. They may be on a three-foot ledge, but they were close.

"Can't say halfway warm. I don't consider soggy and freezing as warm. But I'm not as frozen through with you blocking most of the wind."

"Good to be needed." He carefully maneuvered the ledge,

shifting next to her. "You'll feel better with some food and water in you."

"I doubt that. How's your back?"

"Not bad," he lied, popping the top on a bottle of pain reliever. "Will two of these hurt the baby?"

She took them and washed them down with some water. Guess that answered his question.

"I'm sorry I pushed it last night, Cord."

"Don't apologize. Anyone could have slipped. Important thing is you caught yourself."

"I put the baby in even more danger."

"Don't go there," he warned. Not for himself, but her. He needed the confident Kate. The woman in charge. She couldn't be second-guessing herself.

"I couldn't bear it again," she whispered.

He grabbed her hand and removed the gloves, lacing their fingers together. They'd sat on a mountain before, just like this, the day he asked her to marry him. He knew better than anyone you couldn't go back. Life didn't give do-overs.

"Nothing happened. It worked out." Now wasn't the time to apologize for not protecting her three years ago.

"Oh, good grief, Cord." She took the last sip in the bottle and swallowed her last bite of energy bar. "Can we go now?"

It seemed the way to get Kate to be strong was to get her angry at him. But no matter what, she always wanted to talk. The shrink told him he needed to talk. He disagreed. He knew he'd failed her. Talking about that night wouldn't change anything. Their baby would still be gone.

"Wait."

"Why?" she asked. "Could you come over here? Just stand next to me. We don't have to face each other to talk."

She leaned against the rock face, clearly anxious that he'd been close to the edge. He moved closer, not wanting to cause her more hurt.

"You can't climb as upset as you are."

"I'm not upset, Cord. I mean, I didn't want you to fall, of course. But I'm not upset. You're right. Nothing happened. It's great. So we leave. I wish I could have dried out my socks—"

"My shrink says I need to apologize." He was glad he couldn't see her face. The look of disappointment had to be there. Three years and he wasn't fit for the field.

"You're seeing a shrink?"

"Regulations. I have to be cleared for duty."

"Oh," she said on a deflated sigh. "Why does he think you need to apologize?"

"It's complicated. I just…I just thought I should."

"I don't understand, Cord. What are you apologizing for, the divorce?"

"Why would I? I didn't want it." He crossed his arms, feeling as defensive as he sounded.

"You're right. So what's this apology your psychiatrist thinks you need to make?" She crossed her arms, waiting.

If she gave him an impatient sigh, he'd forget everything he'd thought about saying and just start climbing. He shoved his arms through the straps of the pack to secure it in place. Tilting his gaze, he saw where he'd grip the rocks for a quick escape. As soon as he forced the words out, he needed to get out of there fast. But his shrink had said no phones. For some reason there needed to be eye contact. His, mainly, something about it being more meaningful.

"Aw, hell." He spun her around to look her in the eyes. He kept his hands on her shoulders, but she didn't try to avoid his touch or squirm from his grasp. "I'm sorry I killed our baby girl, Kate. I wasn't there to protect you. I know you hate me for it. I also know you'll never be able to forgive me. I can't forgive myself. I should have told you a long time ago, but I was in the hospital and then it seemed…we…well, I guess I just never had the right words."

BACK INJURY OR NO, her ex-husband Texas Ranger Cord Mc-Crea turned on a dime, knew exactly where he would grab hold and leaped a foot up the rock wall. Kate stared at his jean-covered backside, then the bottoms of his shoes.

He'd thought she hated him because that monster Jorje Serna killed their daughter. She could never hate Cord. Never. And as soon as they stopped again, she'd set him straight.

It took her a bit longer to get started on this last section. She wasn't about to leap to the jutting rocks Cord had grabbed. She was kind of stunned by his sudden urge to finally talk to her. Okay, it was more of a statement than a talk. She got that. But it was Cord! A man who'd never spoken to her about any of that horrible night. He'd listened in silence while she told him what Serna had done. She'd purged all her fear, all of her shame at being so afraid, all her regret at not doing more…and he'd said nothing. Never acknowledged any part of it. She hadn't been certain he'd remained completely awake until his eyes opened, filled with a rage she'd never seen.

"Definitely a start," she said, with him completely out of earshot.

Even with the clear skies, lots of sunlight and no moisture to blink from her eyes, she still moved cautiously. Each move was deliberate and secure. Cord wasn't under her, but from the way he was shooting ahead he had confidence she was fine. At least she didn't feel left behind. It actually reminded her she'd been climbing rocks like this her entire life.

They didn't speak, and soon Cord disappeared over the edge, hopefully back to a trail. Her hands ached but she took time to secure each grip. A couple of minutes went by and she realized Cord hadn't stuck his head over the edge to check on her.

"Cord?" she yelled. "Cord!"

Had he just left her? Nonsense. He'd never do that.

"Kate. Over here." Cord was farther to her left than she'd been looking. But his voice was husky, like a loud whisper. As soon as they made eye contact, he put his finger across his lips.

She reached the ledge and just like the night before, Cord pulled her to the top. And each time, he indicated to remain silent. When he stood, she followed to where he'd dropped the backpack.

"Stay here," he whispered. "No arguing."

Taking off once again without informing her of the plan. What would she do if he ended up shot? She watched as he pulled the machine pistol to his chest and ducked behind a pinyon pine.

What had he seen?

Or heard. The distant whirling of a helicopter bounced around the canyons. Dread, adrenaline and fright all mixed together to put her stomach on edge. She stared in the direction of Cord then peeked over the rock she was backed against. All she saw was another rock.

Forget this. She wouldn't sit on the sidelines and get an update. They were a team. This was her fight, too. She removed her rifle from where it had been strapped to the pack. While she checked for ammo, Cord returned.

"Well?"

"They're searching, but it's the same chopper."

"How can you tell?"

He nodded toward the rifle and grinned. "Bullet holes."

"So what do we do now?"

"I figure it's going to take all day to cross the rest of this plateau and hit Highway 118. They still don't know for certain that we headed this way. May assume we've made it to one of the phones southeast and start to move the drugs."

"We have an advantage since we'll hear the helicopter long before it can see us."

"So we stay hidden from view and head toward the observatory."

"There are places that are closer than that," she pointed out.

"Yeah, but we can't see them. The white domes will give us a line of sight, easier to hit our mark and end up in the right place."

"Easier for our eyes, but not our feet. And how much food did you happen to pack?"

"I'll be okay."

"It's not you I'm thinking about." She grabbed a water bottle from inside the pack, dripped some onto the cuts on her palms.

Watching Cord shift that machine pistol to his back was becoming too natural for her comfort. She really wanted this journey to be over and hiking all the way to McDonald Observatory—while it was their best option—just didn't appeal to her. She wanted to feel safe, but not just on this trip. The longer she was with Cord, the more she wanted him to be involved with the baby. Things were just easier with someone around to help.

Having a child was a new experience. One of those "unknown" things out there that she had no knowledge about.

"Remember the first time I took you to the observatory?" The thought popped into her head along with the hunger for salty nacho chips and artificial cheese. "We got the reservations for the night owl thing, but it was too foggy to see."

Cord knelt next to her, set his hat on the ground and took her palms in his hands. His gentle touch, cleaning the scratches, warmed more than her fingers. He was so familiar. So concerned about even a little thorn in her thumb.

"Isn't that when you were on a natural juice kick and they didn't have anything for you to drink?" he asked.

"I was never high maintenance. I remember you almost drove off a cliff on the way home."

"We were never in danger."

"We had to pull over."

He looked up and shook his head, laughing at her with his eyes. "The fog wasn't the reason we pulled over."

Oh, my. Every inch of her skin tingled. Every molecule was colliding with the one next to it, wanting to jump into Cord's arms. What a night that had been. It started in the car—no, it actually began at his house. A rushed dinner and a drip of salsa landing on her chin.

She'd never been so grateful for fog in her life.

"This one's pretty deep." He skimmed her right palm, close to her wrist. "It's clean, though. Wish I had first aid. Didn't think about it," he said, replacing his hat.

She wanted to tip that old Stetson and let it blow back to Valentine. The desire to mess up his hair while she made love to him on the top of this mountain was overpowering. She couldn't understand it. It was probably one of the most uncomfortable places they'd ever been but, somehow, she felt closer to the man kneeling in front of her.

He stood and took a swig of the water before stowing it in the pack. "You okay? Maybe you should eat an apple."

"Cord, about what you said on the ledge—"

"Forget it. Bad timing."

She couldn't let him walk away. After three years, he'd finally tried to talk. "But I *need* to say something."

He stopped but didn't face her. "Go ahead."

If she went to his side… She wanted to hold his hand or

be held in his arms. She couldn't predict what would happen or prepare for it. How could she?

She was perched on a rock, on top of a mountain, being chased by the Mexican cartel and here's where he'd chosen to talk to her about their little girl. So she stayed where she was…longing to hold his hand and comfort him.

He was finally allowing more than a cover of indifference to show. He was grieving.

The man's timing absolutely stank to high heaven.

Chapter Fourteen

Say it already!

Cord scanned the horizon. That chopper would be back. No question of if, only when. They should be looking for their best way down the other side. They needed an escape route, not a conversation. *Come on, Kate, just say it.*

He could listen to her tell him how much she hated him *and* look for a trail. Keeping his back to her, he moved to the place he'd last seen the chopper. He should have borrowed the binoculars when he'd lifted the ammo and pistol from Burke's gun cabinet.

Trying to look past her, he made the mistake of looking at her. She'd pulled her knees to her chest. No sighing. At least none that he heard. How was he supposed to know what this gesture meant?

"I'm listening, but we have to find a way down. You have to understand."

"Oh, I do." She jumped to her feet, pulled her gear on and joined him.

"I thought you had something you needed to say."

"I'm still debating if you're actually ready to hear it."

"I could quote my shrink if you want. She'd say it's—"

"It's a woman?" she interrupted.

"Yeah, why?"

"I'm just surprised, that's all." Her short inhale and momentary hold of its release told him she was more than surprised. "Go ahead. What would your doctor tell me?"

"She'd *advise* that you can't decide if someone's ready for a confrontation. You can't wait for perfect timing. Things just happen. Life happens."

Kate cocked her head curiously. "All right. No perfect timing. Lord knows, yours certainly wasn't, perched on a four-foot mountain ledge like we were."

"Go on then." He should have listened to himself. Talking was a bad idea.

"You need to believe me. I only blame one person for the death of our daughter. Jorje Serna is a murderer many times over."

"It's easy to say that, Kate. But I know you blame me."

"You blame yourself enough for the both of us, Cord!" Kate yelled. "I'm not angry because you were shot, near dead in a hospital and couldn't be there twenty-four/seven protecting me."

"He wouldn't have come after you—"

"Stop it! Just stop it!" She closed her mouth and began shaking her hands to calm down. "Listen to your own advice and stop thinking you can interpret everyone's thoughts or predict their reactions. I did not divorce you because of the shooting."

"Then why the hell did you?" The words were out quickly, surprising her, if that look was any indication. "I can't remember how many times you said I wasn't there. Didn't you know I couldn't be."

"I knew you were a Texas Ranger when we met. You never hid your career goals. You transferred here because of me. I couldn't and still don't *want* to change you. I loved the man who wears that uniform."

"You divorced me."

"I couldn't do it anymore."

A piece of rock chipped near Kate's boot and flew into the air off the cliff.

"Back." He rushed between her and the open canyon, and they scrambled to where she'd been sitting earlier. "I didn't hear anything. You?"

"No," she whispered. "I'm sorry. We shouldn't have—"

"Shh. Listen."

Quiet.

Then a shot rang out from the distance. Followed by an immediate ricochet.

"He's less than three hundred yards and not a very good shot."

"Probably not, considering the wind," she stated, looking into the canyon between him and the rock. "Or he doesn't *want* to hit us. So do we run or do I cover you?"

"I'm not putting you through that again."

"And I'm not guaranteeing to hit anything, Cord. But I'm good enough to cover you."

"Did you see an animal trail, any logical switchback down?" He dropped his hat on the ground.

She reached for the rifle. "No, we're really limited. We can't go back. There's only forward. We climbed this thing right here because the ridge stretched east and west too far to go around."

She was right. "Forward. I just need to eliminate some speed bumps." He dropped his coat.

"You think the chopper spied us earlier and dropped these guys off?"

"Or they were searching already. One problem at a time." He stuffed Burke's 9mm in the small of his back, dropped an extra clip into his jeans pockets. Pulled the hunting knife and connected its sheath to his belt.

"So what's the plan?"

"Honestly, Kate, I don't have any plan. I'm going to do

my best to find out how many are with the shooter. You stay here to make 'em think we're pinned down. Keep an eye open. Watch your back. You fire a shot for cover, then I'll move."

"What if there are more and they get too close?"

"That's why I'm leaving this." He hung the machine pistol around her neck. "Don't hesitate to just point and shoot."

"For the record, that's a plan," she said, grinning.

"If it makes you feel better to call it that."

It did make her feel better. He could see her relaxed demeanor this time round. Unlike at the canyon the day before. She'd realized he'd tricked her into staying. As he'd left her holding the horses, her eyes had been sparkling, deep bluebonnet-blue. He loved her eyes that way.

He tipped her chin up so their eyes met. Sky-blue. He loved them this color, too. "And for the record, I appreciate you talking to me, so don't think you caused us to get pinned down. *Here* is a lot better to have a face-off than being caught on the side of this mountain with no cover, nowhere to run and no options."

"I hate splitting up, Cord. What if—"

He placed his finger across her lips. "I'll hear you when you yell for me. That's a promise."

If he'd been closer, he would have kissed her. No question. He wanted to assure her he'd be back. He left, leaving her alone with a MAC-10 for protection.

Not the hardest thing he'd ever done...but close.

The only way to get behind the shooter was back the way he'd come along the cliff. Work his way unseen, hanging along the edge for a couple of hundred yards. Keeping his head down, he heard Kate's intake of breath. He couldn't look at her, so behind his back he held up the sign language for "I love you" she'd taught him early in their relationship.

He did. Love her. He'd never stopped. Not since the first

moment they'd met. His first homecoming game back at UT. A chance meeting in the student section. She was with a date in the row in front of him. He was with loud former football players.

His grip slipped and he hung by the dang arm of his weak shoulder. "Dad blast it, keep your mind on what you're doing," he chided himself. He couldn't pull up. He swayed. The pressure on his shoulder threatening to dislocate increased with every movement. He recovered, reaffirmed his right grip and rested the wrenched left side.

Move it. You're losing time!

He could see the ledge where they'd spent the night. The cover he needed was in the opposite direction than they'd climbed this morning. Twenty more yards should do it. Sweat saturated his face but not because of the sun warming his head. The pain in his shoulder and back had been bad before this last climb. Now it was… He couldn't think about it.

Kate needed him. He'd lost track of the shots being fired while he'd dangled in the air. He could still distinguish rifle shots from Kate—different than Serna's crew. Still only one returning fire, though.

That might lean things in their favor. Something going right? What were the chances?

The only way to see how far he'd come was to perform a chin-up. It was going to hurt like hell. Kate fired. He pulled eye level with the ground. Good cover. He just needed up. His muscles shook as he pulled himself to the top. His arm was mush.

There was no time to waste. He'd recover along the way. He didn't know what Kate was shooting at, but he watched the area where her bullet smacked near a gap in the rocks. Sure enough, Serna's crewman returned fire.

He hadn't been raised a huntsman. He hadn't served in

the military. He didn't really have experience moving unseen from one scraggly bush to another. But he loved Kate and would get to that shooter. And he would take him out.

He ducked behind rocks, crawled on his belly and lay frozen to the ground, holding his breath as he unintentionally found the shooter's partner. The second man was crouched several feet below him. Kate was safe from the shooter, but not from the man near him.

No choice who his target was then. He'd lose his surprise advantage on the shooter if he didn't keep this quiet. He let the man pass him, silently unsheathing the blade, flipping it to use the hilt. If he could knock the man unconscious—

Rocks busted apart near his head, shards pricking the back of his hand. Serna's shooter alerted his partner, who stood and leaped at him. The only thing going in their favor was Serna's orders to bring them in alive. Otherwise, he'd have been shot several times over.

The second man trapped his arm—and knife—between their chests. He'd caught this guy by surprise with his gun still in his waistband while they'd been crawling. Cord used his longer legs to wrap around the shorter man and kept him from getting any leverage. He punched the man's head with his weak left hand. He grunted but that was about it. Useless. Another shot, very close to his head.

"Okay, okay. Don't shoot." Cord relaxed his body and released the man's legs. The man shoved up to his knees and gave a sign to the shooter. Cord raised his hands and dropped the knife to the ground near the top of his head.

The man couldn't reach the knife or his weapon without shifting his weight off Cord. When he did, Cord swept up his knife and sliced his side as they both rolled downhill a couple of feet and heard another shot.

He shoved the limp body off him. His blade hadn't killed him, but the sniper had miscalculated, hitting his partner square in the back. Cord used him as cover to get safely to an outcropping.

No radio. No ID. No cell. Nothing on this guy except a gun. He'd either dropped everything with the sniper or they hadn't been prepared to leave the chopper. Now for the sniper and to get back to Kate.

"Cord!"

She was in trouble and her cry shot him through his heart faster than any sniper bullet.

Chapter Fifteen

Face-to-face, looking the stranger in the eyes, seeing the moment of hesitation there. The split-second thought wondering if he saw the same thing on her face flashed in her mind. It wasn't the first time either of them had looked down a gun barrel. She knew that just looking at him.

Serna's man showed his surprise when she didn't pull the trigger. But he also showed confident knowledge that she wouldn't.

One thought merged into the next. Just a split second hesitation. But long enough for the man to jump forward, knock the rifle aside and stick the barrel of his weapon straight under her chin.

That same split second she'd lived before—three years ago—blurred with this one on top of a mountain.

Serna had burst into her living room, having already killed two police officers in front of her home. She'd been petrified and unable to move. It was so unexpected. Serna had wanted her to talk or maybe beg. When she wouldn't, he'd waved the gun around and walked toward the door. He didn't look where he fired his gun. If he had, she'd already be dead. The bullet only caught her in the shoulder, but the resulting trauma caused a miscarriage and killed her baby. She'd lost everything.

The man now shoving the hot barrel into her skin

shouted in Spanish for a comrade's help. There was more gunfire. *Cord!*

What should she do? Fight and take a chance on injuring the baby? *Think logically.* But Serna is anything but logical. You've seen the craziness in his eyes and actions. So you're not dead. This guy didn't pull the trigger straightaway.

Serna wants you alive.

Then I stay alive and wait on Cord. He'll come. He always keeps his promises.

"Jorje, he tell us to bring you alive, but he say nothing 'bout *bambina.*" He kicked the machine pistol away. Knocked the rifle out of reach. "Sit. Hands on head. I keep mouth shut if you not want kick to stomach. *Comprende?*"

She followed his instructions, first shoving loose stones from the site she'd occupy, then crossing her legs to use for protection if needed. She could pull them to her body and maybe stop a direct kick to the baby.

"Hands."

Reluctantly, she put them on top of her head. *Protect the baby* became the mantra in her mind. The last shot might have hit Cord, but she couldn't let the fear take control. Why hadn't he returned yet?

She would not allow herself to become distracted. She could defend herself. Baby or no, she just had to wait for the right moment.

The man tugged the backpack away from her, dumping everything. Never breaking eye contact with her, he rifled through the contents and brought objects between them so he could see what they were. For some reason, she couldn't look away and watched him toss bottled water and fruit over the edge.

Shots echoed among the hills again. Serna's man looked in the direction, the same as her, but there wasn't anything she could do. No weapon close enough, not even a rock large enough to throw. But the sound confirmed Cord was still alive.

After the rapid gunfire, minutes ticked by with nothing, just the wind gusting through the few trees and canyons. A shout in Spanish from a voice stating he was on his way. What had happened to Cord?

The man relaxed and continued his inspection of the backpack. He held up a small bag, and she recognized it as part of what had been under the floor at the lodge. He laughed, pocketed the drugs.

If she didn't have other things to worry about, she might be extremely angry over Cord concealing that he'd removed one. She kept watching, listening for signs of Cord. He might come back the same way he left, but he couldn't execute a surprise. To get to where the sniper was, he'd have to have gone the way this guy had come. So she kept watching, looking for movement of any kind.

"What are we waiting on?" she asked.

"Impatient to meet Jorje?" He laughed again, tossing aside an apple.

"No. Him."

Cord was fifty yards away, rifle to his shoulder, taking aim. The man faced him in time to aim his handgun. Both fired.

As soon as the man toppled sideways, Kate jumped to her feet and ran to Cord, never looking back.

"Sorry that took so long, babe," he said when she was steps away.

She threw herself at him. He lifted her into his arms and she dropped her head on his shoulder.

"I was so frightened. I'm getting really tired not knowing if you're alive or dead."

"I didn't mean for you—"

She didn't need any more words and cut him off with a

kiss. A long, in-depth kiss that couldn't be misinterpreted. Even though she couldn't stay married to him she had to let him know how much he meant to her. While their tongues entwined, she remembered the other close calls he'd had as a Ranger. Were they all like this?

She only had the shooting for a comparison and that had all happened so fast. The hardest part had been dragging Cord into the car to get him to the hospital. He'd been deadweight, unable to use his legs. With every moan, she questioned if she should wait for help.

They'd never know if her dragging him into the car had caused the paralysis or if the bullet was completely responsible. Either way, if she hadn't moved him he would have bled out.

"What's wrong?"

"I'm sorry."

"Yeah, I know. You can't be close to me." He walked away for once. "Well, guess what, Kate? *I can't, either.*"

He's angry? He'd never been angry before.

"It's not that." She needed to explain. She hadn't stopped because she was near him. She'd never told him that she'd been responsible for the paralysis.

"Stay there. You don't need to look at this guy," he commanded.

For once she obeyed without questioning. She knew where the bullet had struck. She'd seen the man's head whip back and closed her eyes before he fell.

"Ah, man, the bastard took my apples."

"He tossed them over the edge." She sank to the ground and drew her knees to her chest.

"You okay?"

"Yeah. Just suddenly exhausted." She crossed her arms and buried her face, blocking the view of Cord with the dead man.

She woke with a start and Cord's hand on her shoulder. No dead guy in sight. "Did I fall asleep?"

"I know, but it's time to get moving." He squatted in front of her, handing her a water bottle and energy bar. "You've had a rough couple of days. I don't blame you for dozing."

"What now?" The dead guy had been covered with his own jacket.

"Well, I'm not sure when the chopper will circle back around for these guys so we should probably get started to the observatory." Cord picked his too-big hat up from the ground and set it on top of her head.

"You think we can make it there without being seen?"

He shrugged and finished off his bar. "We stay under whatever tree cover we can find and we hope for the best."

"There are houses on this side of 118, Cord. They're closer."

"Do you know which way? Heading directly to a white dome I can see from just about any hill around here is a sure thing, a definite direction. We'd be guessing about anything else. It might take even more time if we guess wrong and have to climb one of the hills between those valleys. Not to mention it's flatter where the ranch houses are, less cover than in the canyons."

"I agree." Whether he was seeking her opinion or not, she agreed. At least he'd explained why he'd made the choice. But he wasn't smiling. There wasn't a hint of a smile in his eyes, either.

No matter what happened once they arrived wherever they were going…in the end, Cord McCrea needed to know someone cared and loved him. He couldn't go through life like this current whitewashed version.

He stood, offered his hand and pulled her to her feet. Pack on his back, carrying the remaining water, energy bars and all the weapons, he led the way around another jut of rocks.

"Want your hat?" she asked.

"You need it worse than me. You're already burned from the sun you got yesterday."

She hadn't been. Not really. But she wasn't going to argue. She appreciated the shade. The sun was bright in the sky and they had a long walk ahead. "You can see the front coming from the northwest. Think we've got time?"

"I don't think we have a choice."

"Are you going to tell me what happened with the sniper? Or why you think the men were in the helicopter?" Did she really want to know the answers?

"None of them had survivor gear, just weapons."

"So the helicopter dropped off two guys to wait on us and just flew away?"

"Three. That's why I was late."

Three dead men. He'd fought and killed three men today. Three yesterday.

"Don't do that, Kathleen."

"What do you *think* I'm doing?"

"I know you're thinking about the men who died. But you can't think of them as men. They're drug runners and murderers. Would-be executioners delivering us to Serna." He faced her. "They're part of the gang and may have been the actual scum who put a gun to our friends' heads and pulled the trigger."

"Stop! I get it." She threw up her hands, wanting to cover her ears and block the images from her mind.

"No, you don't." He grabbed her shoulders, giving her the slightest of shakes. He pulled the pistol from the back of his waist and handed it to her. "Next time, don't hesitate—pull the damn trigger. Shoot the son of a bitch before he gets close enough for you to see what color his eyes are."

He didn't apologize and she didn't ask him to. Because she'd hesitated, they might have been captured. As much as she worried about him while he was gone, he worried about her. He'd showed her an "I love you" hand. The only word he knew in sign language.

He walked away from her, down the hill in a direct line to the observatory. They might just make it sometime today at this pace. If she could keep up and if Serna's men didn't find them. This side of the mountain was less rocky. Better for grazing. Easier to walk. She just wished it was easier to believe they'd actually make it out of this alive.

DAMN, WET WEATHER. The drugs and weapons had been tediously moved to a second location as soon as the storm had let up. Slower, without the benefit of the ATVs. Both engines had seized. His guess was dirt in the gas. And damn Mc-Crea for figuring out it was the easiest way to completely halt the vehicles.

They'd barely moved the last of the shipment before the DEA had shown up and begun their search. He'd been gone all night and it was time to get back to work preparing for a doozy of a snow front. He cranked the heat up a notch, hoping that the McCreas didn't have the luxury.

God, he hated them. It didn't matter what their last names were. They were all from the same cloth. Men who thought they knew more than anyone else. Men who told you to suck it up and let your family sink into a mire. Holier-than-thou men who needed to be brought down several notches so they could be walked on for a while.

Yeah, he hated them.

And pretty damn soon…they'd be hating him.

Chapter Sixteen

"All right. I give in. I don't want to do this anymore." Kate stopped near a semiflat boulder and sat.

She'd tried to clarify herself each time they'd rested. As soon as the words "what I meant" got past her lips, he was gone. So she hadn't been able to explain about the kiss. She'd had no luck getting Cord to listen.

"You need to stop again?"

"Again? I think we've walked for a couple of hours since the last rest, but that's not what I'm talking about." She understood the silence when they didn't know if Serna's men were nearby. She especially understood the need to conserve their energy while they were hiking up and down hills without any solid path under their feet. It took concentration that was becoming more difficult to obtain with each tiring step.

But there hadn't been a sign of another human since early this morning and Cord still wasn't answering her. He conveniently couldn't hear and asked her to repeat herself or he left and just never gave her the chance to finish.

"Actually, it's only been forty-five minutes," he said, passing the water to her.

"Right. Where are you going now?" That's the action she didn't understand—his running off. He wouldn't give her the opportunity to discuss anything that had happened.

"I need to look ahead."

"But you haven't eaten. You've barely had any water. And you aren't resting. You keep running up hills and coming back when I'm ready to go. You don't even drop the pack, so your back must feel horrible."

He pressed his lips together and shrugged. Shrugged and left.

Cord ran up the hill, blending into the lone tree trunk at the top. He stared in every direction for three or four minutes—or at least it felt like three or four minutes to her. Time seemed to be crawling by as they hiked to the observatory. Her protector came back from each of his uphill runs to give them a new landmark to aim for and keep them on track.

The pace he set didn't bother her. Cord's abandoning her each time she spoke did. She'd been so hopeful they were actually getting closer to discussing what had happened and why she'd gone through with the divorce. She hadn't been able to explain where her mind had wandered during the last kiss. As a result, he'd shut completely down. Withdrawn. Spoke to her only when needed.

"Everything looks clear," he said, hurrying down the hill. "We're in luck."

"Really?"

"Yeah. One of those houses you mentioned is just over that rise in the valley. Didn't see any cars or horses, but we can call for help."

"It might be one of the observatory people. I don't think there are any ranches this close to the state park."

"Doesn't matter as long as they have a phone. Let's go."

He took her hand and brought her to her feet. A gesture that would have brought her straight into his arms before the shooting. She missed the closeness, the love, the dependability. She even missed the dirty dishes and laundry and house cleaning. She held tight to his hand. He tossed a short questioning glance her way but didn't let go.

The closer they got to the house, the more apparent it became that it had been abandoned for some time. No satellite dish, no wires leading to the house. There was a windmill for an empty cistern, but it wasn't turning.

"We must be farther away from the road than I thought," she said as they crossed through an unlocked finished door into a half-finished building. Rock and wooden outside walls, a stone fireplace, a nice wood floor, some electrical wire and nothing else. The drywall sat covered in a far corner with visible dust caked on top of the tarp.

"Looks like someone began building this place and gave up on the idea a while ago."

"Shoot. That means no phone."

"No lights," he returned.

"No motorcar," she sang.

"Not a single luxury," they sang together, and laughed at the impromptu *Gilligan's Island* theme.

"Oh, that was funny." She caught her breath. "So I guess you're the thrifty professor. Can you whip us up a makeshift communication device with that portable radio?"

"And since you're Mary Ann—"

"Not Ginger?" She tried a movie-star pout, but began laughing again.

Cord grabbed her coat as she removed it and placed a hand on her stomach. "This has more of a Mary Ann feel to me. Besides, you're an awesome cook. Definitely a Mary Ann."

He shrugged out of her father's coat and glanced into the other rooms. All had doorways to the living area, but no doors. She crunched newspapers that were a couple of months old and dropped them in the fireplace.

"Food?" she asked.

"No kitchen appliances, empty cabinets."

"So do we push forward or hang out here awhile? I vote

for defrosting my digits." She wiggled her fingers and rubbed her hands together. A fire would be nice since she hadn't really been warm since the car. "I don't know about you, but I'd love to dry my socks."

"I think there's enough stuff here to get a fire going. Nothing suspicious about a house sporting a fire. We can warm up a bit before we head out." He walked over to the fireplace. "And you can dry your socks after the fire warms up the room. Deal?"

"Deal. How long do you think we have? Maybe Serna has all his men tied up fighting the DEA. They should have found that cave hours ago, right?"

"We can only hope they were all at the cave and got locked up. Somehow I don't think that happened." He disappeared around a corner, came back with two bags containing camp chairs. "I think Serna and his men have had a fairly good warning system in place for years. The cave was loaded with supplies and crates. I wish I'd had time to look inside. But with that amount of supplies, I'd assume he was confident of not being found."

"Always the Ranger. Is that the reason you stashed a bag of drugs in your pack?"

Wrong thing to ask. He didn't look sheepish or sorry for not telling her he'd taken the bag. "Can you blame me for wanting to put this guy away? We were so close to shutting him down, Kate."

"But it doesn't matter. None of it matters. Can't you see that? He was in a federal prison for three years. Three years and that bag's the proof nothing slowed his operation. He's not threatened by you. And he wouldn't think twice about you right now or the Rangers or the DEA if you hadn't defended me and killed his brother."

"You asking me to walk away again?"

Answering his question would lead to another round of

fighting and she just didn't have the strength. She couldn't explain about the kiss, either, and barely remembered why it was important to tell him. "Is that one a cot? Trade you."

He accepted her change of subject and unfolded the cot. "Lie down and I'll get that fire going."

"Orders. Orders. Orders. Oh, wow." Taking the pressure off her legs and back muscles was heavenly. "This is almost as good as the Burke's guest bed."

"Better than last night's ledge?"

She rolled onto her side to watch him build the fire and light it with a fireplace lighter he'd found in the kitchen. "This is sad."

"What is, babe?"

"This house is someone's dream and they had to walk away from it."

"Sort of fitting then."

"What do you mean?" She thought she knew and shouldn't have asked. She didn't want their dream to be over. She rubbed her belly, hoping he wouldn't say the words aloud.

"Sort of like us," he whispered. "Get some rest. I'm going to look around, keep watch and see 'bout some more wood." He pulled her father's old coat on across his broad shoulders and quietly shut the door behind him.

Kate didn't know if he was sad, too, but she finally cried. An exhausted, hungry weeping for everything. She closed her eyes and wanted to dream about a nice, safe world with no Jorje Serna or other horrible men chasing them over a mountain.

CORD PULLED THE door closed as quickly and gently as possible when he saw Kate was asleep. His stomach rumbled loudly, but there was nothing to eat. He was saving the last apple and energy bar for when she woke up. She needed them more than he did.

He threw some wood chips on the fire, got it going a bit stronger and threw on some dead branches. The place was warming nicely, but he added his jacket on top of Kate. His back screamed at him. His left hand still had sharp twinges and was tingling as if it was asleep. *Not good.*

Rest. They both needed it and there was nothing else he could do. He moved the chair and propped his feet on the low hearth. Man, it felt good to sit and just relieve the pressure on his back awhile.

It would be a nice house if it ever got finished. The fireplace was made from stones they'd probably found clearing the land. Nothing fancy, just sturdy. So were the walls.

"Such a shame," Kate said softly. "I mean the house. Left unfinished, it's sort of lonely."

"It's got a lot of potential. Whoever built it put in a lot of time and craftsmanship." He twisted in the chair to look at her and couldn't hide the grunt of pain his back caused.

"Why don't you lie down awhile and stretch your back? It must be aching terribly. Come on, we need you to be able to move and get us out of here."

She stood and was already sighing a long exasperated one that meant she thought he wouldn't listen to her.

"I can take the floor."

"Fine. Be that way. But I'm ready to sit now and won't be using the cot."

She wouldn't. Stubborn, beautiful woman. And she was right. He did need to be able to move. Kate's hand was outstretched, ready to help him. He took it, determined to stand and drop her cool, silky skin as fast as he could.

And then she smiled.

Damn, she was beautiful.

In that instant he wanted her something fierce and didn't

know if he could walk away. The need grabbed every manly part of him, including his heart. His insides shook. His breathing stopped when he saw the same hunger in her eyes.

He couldn't drop her hand. Instead, he drew her to him. He needed to kiss her and not be turned away. This time— if there was a this time—he wouldn't be pushed away. She came to him, her body pressing to him, tilting her chin slightly in the air, ready for his lips to claim hers.

"Don't kiss me if— I won't stop this time, Kate."

"I don't want you to."

He kissed her, starving for her closeness. He wrapped his arms around her back and anchored her to him. It wasn't enough.

"Not enough."

"Mmm."

A yes? He couldn't tell, but it wasn't a no. As much as he wanted her to stay warm, he wanted her out of that Tech sweatshirt. Wanted Burke out of the picture. Wanted anyone else out of the picture permanently. He grabbed the edges and broke their kiss long enough to pull it over her head and throw it to the far side of the room.

Her work shirt was there and then gone along with his own. She'd seen the scars and hadn't turned away. She touched the entry wound and slowly moved her hands to either side of his neck and rough, whiskered cheeks.

Her fingers then pushed through his hair, pulling his mouth back to hers. Long, excited kisses, her teeth nipping at his bottom lip, drinking in her taste, needing more. Always wanting more.

Her fingertips circled the nipples on his chest, hardened from the cold or stimulation, he didn't care. He just didn't want it to stop. Any of it. But he needed more.

Needed her.

Her hands dropped to his belt. If she got her way, this

would be over way too quickly. He tugged her thermals up and off and immediately went for her pants. He slid his hands inside the waistband, easy to do with the snap already popped for her belly's comfort. She'd already kicked off her boots when she lay down, and he used his foot to push the pants to the floor for her to step out of.

It was a dance they'd done before. He'd seen her beautifully naked in front of him hundreds of times. But never like this. Her breasts were swollen, spilling over the lace of her bra. He brushed the back of his hands across the dark pink of a nipple, watched it pucker under his touch, watched her body shiver with delight.

The overlarge coat she constantly wore, and even the granny nightshirt from the day before, hid the gentle swell of their child. Without her clothes, the baby bump was just as real as the kick.

Backlit by the glowing fire, he twisted his hand in her hair, bringing her back to his mouth. He splayed his free hand across her belly hoping to feel the baby move again.

Everything about Kate made him want her more. How was that possible? How had he stayed away from her all this time? She was so much a part of him, he didn't know how he functioned without her near.

That was the thing…he'd only been sleepwalking through life without her. But being near him was dangerous—for her and the baby. He stilled his hands, wondering if making love to Kate was the right thing to do.

"Don't you dare change your mind, Cord McCrea." She tugged on his chin until he looked in her eyes. "I'm so hot for you at this very minute, I'm about to explode."

No mind reading necessary. She just knew him and could read his body language before it caught up with what he was thinking. She reached behind her back, and her bra fell to the floor.

"Well?" she asked.

Did she really expect him to put words to how he felt?

He couldn't talk so he showed her by kissing as much of her pale skin as he could. She quivered in his arms as he laid her on the cot. He had to sit in the chair to get his shoes off. She laughed at him the entire frustrating time. The larger borrowed jeans were easily kicked to the floor as he stood and stopped just short of jumping on top of her.

"You're so beautiful, Kate."

"But will you still think so four months from now?" She smiled, teasing him with an image of her at full term.

"I can't think of anything prettier." Her skin had cooled and he lay on top of her to warm her back up. "You're sure about this? I know what our bodies want, babe, but—"

"Shh. No thinking. No rationalizing. Just love me."

I do and always will.

Chapter Seventeen

Kate did nothing but feel. She'd wanted to be with Cord since the moment she'd seen him at the fencerow. For the moment, it didn't matter what was happening in the world that threatened them. There was just his naked body on top of hers. Just his strong hands skimming her sensitive skin, rediscovering the new curves she'd developed.

"I could get used to these," he said as he cupped the additional size of her breasts.

She didn't want to think about the future, that making love to him might be for the last time. Even when they'd conceived the baby, she hadn't believed it would be the final time. They still loved each other, didn't they? Love had never been their problem.

Serna was the problem and Cord was right. The madman would never stop until she was dead. He wanted to punish Cord by hurting her.

Stop it. Don't think. Just feel.

Cord's fingertips explored, stimulated and gave her courage to caress his skin. Even when she skimmed over his scars, he jumped slightly but didn't pull away.

"Does it still hurt?" She circled the bullet scar, more worried about the new bruises beginning to show on his ribs.

"They tell me it doesn't."

"But?"

"Don't worry about it."

He sealed his lips against hers, successfully stopping any words she might have said. Successfully stopping any thoughts except how much she loved being in his arms. And how much she wanted him inside her.

She shifted, moving him more into the V of her legs. His hand drifted between them, driving her to a crazy explosion. "Cord!"

She didn't need to say more. He captured her mouth again and joined their bodies at the same time. She was just as much a part of him as he was her. She knew it. Saw the connection in his eyes. Wanted to keep it forever. They climaxed together.

"I love doing that to you," she said, grabbing his biceps and attempting to get him to relax a moment. "Stay."

"I don't think so. I might pass out. We shouldn't have—"

"Please don't tell me how it was wrong. I don't have any regrets about what we did. You shouldn't, either."

He jumped up and draped her coat on top of her. He pulled his boxers and jeans on in one fell swoop. Then he was sitting and lacing up those Ranger-code shoes. "Get dressed before you fall asleep, babe." He shoved his arms into his coat and strode to the door. "I need to look around before we head out. It might be a while."

Kate's heart was still pushing the blood through her veins double time. She could feel the beating in her throat. She'd hardly caught her breath before Cord was out the door with her staring after.

She got dressed and took the time to braid her hair to keep it out of her way. She placed more wood on the fire, moved the cot a bit closer and lay back down. It seemed that she'd just closed her eyes when Cord gently shook her shoulder to wake her, but it was definitely colder and darker in the room.

"You ready?" he asked.

"There's snow on your jacket." She grabbed his bare hands he held near the fire, immediately warming them between her own. "You're like ice."

"I found the road. We should be able to make it to the observatory by seven or eight." He gently removed his hands from hers in order to rotate his body in front of the dying fire.

"What's going on?" She stood, shoving the cot backward with the force.

"Nothing. I'm just trying to get us out of here. We can't stay with no food or water. The only choice is to brave the storm for two, maybe three hours tops."

"Is that why you left in such a hurry?"

"Babe—" He stopped himself, probably because of the look on her face at his endearment. "It was irresponsible of me to make love to you here. I don't know where Serna's men are and you are far from safe."

"Bull hockey. You ran out that door and away from me. Were you trying to pay me back for leaving you like I did five months ago?"

"What?"

"How are we ever going to move past any of that if we keep—"

"There is no moving past anything, Kate. Get used to the idea. Lord knows I had to." He slammed his hat back on his head and slammed the door behind him.

She smothered the remaining fire, slid the chairs back into their bags and returned them to the counter.

She gave the living room a longing look when the blast of cold air hit her face. She secured the door and searched for Cord while wrapping her scarf around her face for a bit of protection. She also pulled on her work gloves over the smaller knit gloves that had been sufficient earlier.

"It wasn't so cold when the sun was shining. Guess the

front they've been talking about finally hit in full force," she said.

"Guess so." He removed his hat and shoved it on top of her knit cap.

She wasn't going to argue with him. It wouldn't do any good and he'd just run up a hill or something again.

"We're using the road?" she asked like an idiot after the third or fourth step toward the two rain-filled tire treks the owner hadn't used in quite some time.

"It's an easier hike unless you think we should climb the two or three hills between here and 118."

"If you're certain it's safe."

"We're out in the open either way."

"Then we better get started."

One foot in front of the other. One step at a time. They made it to the main road in less than an hour. Pretty good time for two exhausted and starving souls. It was too difficult to actually hold a conversation, but it wasn't difficult to think about what she'd like to say.

Even if they'd wanted to hitchhike, no one was out greeting this hard-blowing storm front. But just in case Serna's men were driving the area, they chose a safe place to cross to the north side of 118.

"I can almost taste the cheesy nachos at their snack bar," she whispered on the other side.

"You can't stand those things."

"That was before." She patted the baby. "Really. I can practically smell them. And if I don't get them, I'm going to be whining a long time."

"You don't whine, either."

"Yes, I do. A lot."

That got her a relaxed smile and a soft knock on the brim of his hat.

They stayed close to the road, not having much choice

since the terrain was steep and difficult. They hadn't seen a soul since the shoot-out this morning. Chances were that Serna was completely out of the area, since the DEA had planned to raid the lodge.

"I hear a car. Let's get off the road. Now."

They took cover about twenty yards uphill by diving behind several juniper trees on the downhill slope. She bent down and he covered her with an arm, keeping her face toward the ground.

She didn't see anything, just heard a car pass above their heads. "It didn't slow down. Sure wish we could get a ride the rest of the way."

They stood, brushing the snow and slush from their pants.

"Fifteen minutes and those nachos are all yours," Cord said, helping her step onto the road.

"I'd give them up in a heartbeat just to have a heater gusting hot air onto my toes. What's the plan? Who will you call to pick us up?"

"I was hoping to call in a favor, but this snow is making any plan impossible."

"As long as we get some food first. Nachos, a hamburger, maybe some French fries—oh, wow, I really want fries now and a great big cup of hot chocolate."

"What's with you and the junk food? Wait—do you hear that?"

"It's just another car. It might even be the same one if the observatory's closed."

"Too soon." He waved at her to get back to the juniper. "It's the same one, I recognize the muffler."

She slid downhill on her bottom, the cold slush seeping through her jeans. This time, Cord stayed closer to the road, gun drawn as the car zoomed downhill toward them.

"Stay there," he shouted.

"No way."

"Come on, Kate. Listen to me and stay there."

The car was upon them and she couldn't shimmy up that slope on her own anyway. So she stayed wedged between two tree trunks to keep herself from slipping farther down the incline. The snow had combined with the earlier rain and the ground was just slick mush. But stuck where she was, she couldn't see a darn thing.

A weapon discharged and she instinctively ducked. Then another. Rapid fire from another point, single shots from above her. "Cord!"

"We've gotta run for the observatory."

"Right." She tugged on her boot, now stuck inches off the ground. "Dear Lord, help me."

"Can you find a route up?" He sounded anxious, worried.

She couldn't bring herself to distract him by saying she was stuck. *Calm down, look at it and get this done.* She removed her right foot, twisted a bit and dug her boot heel into the mud. The gunfire was less frequent but she still jerked at every discharge. With her weight on her free foot, she pushed at the small tree trunk until she could pull free, careful not to slip the other ten feet to the bottom of the gully.

"Kathleen?"

She looked up the slope. It was impossible without him pulling her like before. Maybe on a different day she could have, but now she just didn't have the strength to do it herself after walking the past three hours.

"I can't—"

The gunfire was closer. She swung herself around the juniper to see if there was another way up. The quickest way to safety was on the road. They were minutes away from the twenty-four-hour staff at the observatory. If they had to climb…even the idea of having to climb more, especially alone. She just felt defeated.

Cord slid down the hill, reaching out to catch the trees

with his good arm. "Start running, woman! Let's get out of here before they notice I'm gone."

"Down?"

"Looks like the only way." He took the lead and she fell in close behind.

They hit the narrow but basically level gully. Knee-deep in water they ran, keeping the road to their right. It might have been the hardest part of the entire past three days. Her knees burned. Her overworked thigh muscles were screaming at her for rest. Her throat was so dry she wanted to catch snowflakes for moisture.

Cord held up his hand for her to stop. She bent forward, resting on those worn-out knees while he shimmied up the embankment, took a quick look and then returned. Where did he pull that energy from?

"It looks like," he whispered, his frosty breath coming in spurts as he rested, "we're about two hundred yards from the entrance."

"Then it's another quarter mile to find a human at this time of night."

"Remember those drainage pipes under the main road to the parking lot?"

"Where I just had to have our picture taken in front of the century plant?"

"Right. You can stay there while I find help."

"Normally, I'd argue with you, but my legs are like Jell-O and I wouldn't be able to keep up. So we go about four hundred yards, climb up, cross the road, use the trees for cover until the parking lot. Then we just hope no one sees us run another hundred yards to drainage pipes we hope have already drained."

"Sounds like a plan."

She laughed, caught herself, clapping a gloved hand over her mouth and watched Cord smile in spite of their dire situation. She put her hands on either side of his face and pulled his lips to hers.

"Let's go," she said quickly. "I've waited years to lie in a slush-filled drainage pipe."

Chapter Eighteen

"You are one smart man," Serna told him, slapping him on the shoulder and tucking his phone in his pants pocket.

He hated the slap. And hated the fake camaraderie he tolerated from Serna. He wasn't like these men. He had really begun hating the so-called man walking around the empty bunkhouse. He wished he could get rid of him, but he was an important part of the Danver downfall. A downfall that would only happen if the idiot's people could catch Kate and Cord.

"Since your boys haven't checked in, they probably went head-to-head with McCrea." He leaned against his favorite post near the door. "I told you the only place those two could be headed was toward the observatory. They're smart."

Serna appeared to be high again. Pacing the room, stumbling over his own toes. "How long will it take to get there?"

"From here?" He rubbed his chin, contemplating. "The roads are going to be slick. On a normal day it might be a couple of hours. With the snowfall? Add another hour or so."

"I can't wait that long," Serna hissed through a broken tooth he'd received in prison. "Take me to the chopper."

"You're going to fly? Visibility is almost nil and the DEA is all over our asses."

Serna pulled his gun quickly for a man with such shaky

hands. "Go for it, *amigo*. It saves me a lot of trouble later, I'm thinking."

His own gun was still behind his back and not a risk he wanted to take at the moment. "I can drive you to the chopper. No one will miss me."

"No. They won't." Serna dialed, talking in Spanish, most likely to his pilot.

Maybe they'd crash into a mountain.

IT TOOK A few minutes before the men in the white car stopped shooting. Cord could hear them driving back and forth along the road. "The bastards are too lazy to look for us down here."

"And I'm very grateful they are," Kate said, breathing hard and resting by leaning on her knees. "I'm *so* tired."

"How are your socks?" he teased. They were both soaked again, making their legs weigh a ton, making the walk through the water runoff even more difficult.

"Wet." She smiled and started picking her way through the brush. "Come on, Ranger Boy."

"That's my girl," he muttered to himself. Kate never gave up.

He knew she was exhausted. Heck, he could barely move. Even though they were wet, starving, aching and ready to sleep for a week, she didn't complain, didn't whine and just kept pushing forward. Those nachos—processed cheese and all—were looking pretty darn good to him, too.

The ravine followed the direction of the road fairly closely and they'd completed another turn. It should be the last before it straightened out and they could head straight for the parking lot.

Time to check things out. He stopped and watched Kate bend forward, stretching her back. He knew that sign of pain all too well. He pulled her within his arms, massaging her lower back muscles through her coat.

"I think it's been a bit longer than fifteen minutes."

"I haven't heard the car in a while and need to check our bearings. I need you to wait here," he whispered. "Take the pistol. I'll call like a dove when I come back. Shoot anything else that moves."

She nodded and he let her go. He saw a dead log and helped Kate climb halfway up the hill. She took the gun and he left. He didn't like leaving her alone. She was shivering and they needed shelter, so he couldn't delay. Down to their last option. No food, more snow and just plain exhaustion were almost worse enemies than Serna.

The men in the car were parked at the entrance and waiting on the warm hood. They all seemed underdressed and ill prepared for the cold weather. A note for the investigator in him. These men had come from a warmer climate and hadn't planned on staying long. Perhaps chasing him hadn't been in their plans, either. More important, why had two men apparently so unfamiliar with the terrain been waiting for them on the observatory road?

If Kate weren't with him, it would be the first question he'd ask after he took them into custody. Someone local was helping them. Burke? Juan? It had to be a local rancher who knew about the lodge. Someone who knew the Danvers weren't utilizing that section of their land. He knew Juan, and the more he'd thought about it, he just didn't have the spending habits of someone trafficking drugs. So what was really going on?

He stored the information for later. His first priority was getting Kate and the baby to safety. Then he'd come back and seek the answers to his questions. He followed the path to his ex-wife—a status that was getting harder and harder to remember—and whistled like a dove. He didn't need to be shot again.

She kept the gun pointing in his direction, looking past him to verify he was alone. *Yep, that's my girl.* "Getting around the bozos checking their cell phones won't be all that difficult."

"But?"

"But I couldn't see any cars in the parking lot. Activities have probably been canceled due to the weather," he answered, and sat on the log next to her.

"It's probably a skeleton crew here tonight and there are a lot of telescopes farther up the mountain," she finished on a long sigh.

"Right."

"So I hide."

"Take my coat." He pulled off her father's coat and pushed it in her hands.

"It's snowing again."

"I'll run faster and work up a sweat. Don't worry about me being warm. You two are the ones who will be stuck in a wet drainage pipe."

Her hands went protectively over the baby. He helped get her father's coat on over her own, tucked some stray blond wisps inside her cap and wrapped her in his arms.

"We can do this, right?" Her voice sounded small and uncertain, and a tear fell from the corner of her eye.

It hurt to see her cry. "No doubts."

But he did have doubts. The McDonald Observatory had worked hard to keep the man-made light to a minimum for the telescopes. With no moon there was no way to see where a car might be. He had to physically check out all the parking lots until he found a person on duty.

They stood and his back protested with a stab of pain.

He wanted to cry out with each step. He bit his lip—hard—to keep his mouth from admitting something was wrong. Kate couldn't know.

Running. Lord give him strength.

He led the way uphill and around the buffoons still sitting on the car hood, waiting. Not the brightest bulbs in the pack. He and Kate had just hiked country that included a mountain range, and successfully avoided these nimrods by walking through the rain runoff. They entered the facility on the south side. No cars in the lot. No cover to protect them.

"How long do you think they'll sit there waiting for us to stroll up the drive?"

"Head that way." She pointed east. "There's an eight-foot brick wall by the visitor center that will hide us if they drive into the parking lot. Or we can head around back."

"That's not toward your hiding place."

"I've got a deal for you, Ranger." She darted in front of him, clearly with a second wind, heading to the back of the visitor center.

"And I've got a bad feeling about this."

Cord followed. They were behind the wall. Kate led him directly to an employee entrance door. A glass door.

He pulled on the door. Locked. Just as he suspected.

"Oh, for goodness' sake, Cord. Stop thinking like a law-abiding citizen." She flipped him around and took the rifle from its spot on the side of the pack. "Step back."

She waited for him and used the butt of the rifle against the glass.

"What are you doing?"

"Going inside."

"They'll hear the alarms."

"Yes, everyone will, including the staff."

Kathleen Danver McCrea would always be smarter than him.

"Ah, GOT IT. Everyone hears and I don't have to waste time running all over the mountain looking for nachos—or a phone."

Cord made her laugh. Now. Freezing, stranded in the snow, starving, men trying to kill them, and Cord made her laugh. And the thought of those nachos just made her want them all the more.

"Okay. Let's get this door open so you don't have to run all over the mountain looking for food." She swung back to hit the door again and he raised his hand to stop her.

"Wait. Let's think about what's going to happen."

"You want to make a plan?" she asked, excited that he'd made more than one with her over the past several days.

"I know, I know. Don't fall over. Our plans seem to be working out. I just think this is one of those times we need to walk through all the possibilities." He walked to the end of the wall.

"I agree. Can you see them?"

"No. Serna's men will get here before the staff. Stay inside until the sheriff gets here. Then call Paul Maddox and ask for an immediate evac."

"Got it. What will you be doing?"

"Getting rid of Serna's men. If I can get above them, I should be able to keep them out of the building. But if they get past me, we need to check the other entrances and see if this is the best to defend. We'll also have to deal with any staff who come down to check out the alarm."

"We'll need to make certain they can't be used as hostages. You'll need your coat back." She lifted her arm, indicating for him to tug the sleeve.

"Keep it for now. Keeping them from grabbing hostages means taking Serna's men out first."

"Cord?"

"Hmm?" He led the way around the building.

"Both of those men were checking their cell phones. Do you think they've already told Serna where we are?"

He didn't need to answer. The look on his face said it all. "We can do this, Kate."

"So he's on his way then. You can't be certain. They may try to take us to him."

"Either way, this ends tonight. The two idiots who expect us to cross the street in front of them seem to be waiting on reinforcements."

"We can't endanger anyone working here." She grabbed his upper arm and spun toward him. "And if we break into this building we'll be doing just that."

"I'll have an advantage from the roof that I can't get anywhere else. I could catch these guys while they're still in their car. We can barricade the door and wait on reinforcements."

"And if you can't eliminate all your targets? What then? Can you guarantee they won't grab the staff who will show up when the alarm sounds? What if they're caught in the crossfire?"

"So we're back to the original plan. You hide. I find the staff and get a phone."

"Or we work together to take out those two men and use their car to find help."

"That's too risky."

"We can do this, Cord. It's the best solution. The only way we can control what those men do is to take them out of the equation." She saw in his eyes that he was weighing the possible outcomes. "We work well together. We always have."

And it wasn't hard to recognize that he'd included her in the decision-making process. A first. He'd listened.

"Same as before. You stay back. Cover me with the rifle."

"If we're lucky, they're still waiting."

IF THERE WAS one thing Cord could count on it was not being lucky. Luck hadn't really been on their side for the past three years.

They made the decision to take the two men out quietly at the main road, but as they began to move, the car circled through the parking lot with its lights off. They heard the muffler and ran back to the brick wall to find where they were stopping.

"They're patrolling? Why?" he asked.

"Maybe we should just hide? Together. It will take Serna a couple of hours to get here. We could make it back to the tree line and—"

Cord took her by the shoulders and shook his head. "You're forgetting he has access to a chopper. Our friends are probably driving around. They want to look busy because he's almost here."

"Then we definitely need to find the staff and call—"

"It's too late. We're it. Hear that?" He pointed to the sky. "Not thunder. It's a chopper."

He paced. Three steps away from her and three steps back. All the while shoving the snow off his head, tugging at his short hair. Worried. And if she didn't know him so well, she probably wouldn't have seen the fright in his eyes he was attempting to hide.

"Which plan do you want to go with?" she asked, reaching out and grabbing his hand. The strength she needed flowed into her even through their gloved fingers.

"We head back to the woods. Circle around and take the car when they're not looking."

"Sounds good. Just wish it included a good steak and cheesy potatoes."

"That kid must love cheese," he teased.

"Naw, this is all me. You know I'm a meat-and-potatoes gal."

"I've seen you eat your fair share of crab legs."

"Oh, my gosh, those were good crab legs," she whispered, gaining a crooked smile from her ex-husband.

They waited for the car to head to the north side of the facility before they ran. Blending into the trees toward the south, the sounds of the helicopter grew louder.

"We need to warn the staff."

"I'll do my best, Kate, but I haven't got many options." His low, soft voice shook through her as he checked the weapons and palmed the remaining bullets for his pistol.

He was right. They were low on ammo and if it came down to a fistfight, Cord was injured and exhausted. His upper-body strength was amazing, but in his current state, she just didn't know how long he'd last.

"You need to go Rambo on these guys."

"What do you mean?"

"Cull them from the herd and take 'em out one by one."

"This isn't a movie, babe. I can be prosecuted for something like that."

She could see the possibilities crowding his brain. Normally she'd think he was cute raising one corner of his mouth and barely shaking off a bad idea, then processing another. Today she was glad he was considering it. Not stating aloud how he planned to eliminate the men determined to kill them was just fine with her. He handed her the rifle again.

The chopper topped the trees over their heads. The wind stirred the snow in a circular pattern; the running lights gave the white flakes an eerie glow as they swirled faster for a few seconds. Fortunately, the evergreens they were standing under protected their location, but they were out of time.

"Don't, Cord. I know that look." She already knew he would go back and make a stand alone. There was nothing she could do to stop him. His mind was set on one plan of action.

"It's the only way." He handed her the pack to hold while he took all the ammunition. "And don't double back and try to help me."

"It's better when we're together."

He raised his eyebrows, clearly thinking of their time together that morning. Then his lips flattened, all serious. "Don't be afraid, babe."

She was terrified. How could she be anything but? "What do you want me to do?"

"You'll be hidden in the trees all the way up the south side to the telescope. It's a longer haul. Steeper, harder, so take your time."

"Won't the observatory people come to see who's in the helicopter landing on their lawn? Take your coat back and don't argue. You need it."

"I'll do my best to keep them safe." He tugged the sleeves off and slipped back into her father's coat.

"If they're here, then why in the world are you sending me up the hill to fetch them?"

"My turn to fight." He pulled the collar up on her coat and tucked the scarf inside. Once again, he squashed his huge Stetson on top of her head. "No matter what you hear going on, Kate, I can't do what I need to do if you come back. I need you safe."

She kissed him. Or he kissed her. It didn't matter. None of their problems mattered. It would be a miracle if they got out of this alive. So she kissed him again. Long and hard, then soft and sweet.

"I'm sorry I went through with the divorce, Cord. I should have stood by you."

"Come on now, Kate. There's nothing in our song about

failure. I got this covered." He gave her cheek a sweet caress and left his footprints in the freshly fallen snow as he returned to face their demons.

Chapter Nineteen

"Ranger McCrea. Let's get this over with. No reason to hide longer. I know you are here."

Jorje Serna.

So the drug-running bastard had come himself. If they were in the same chopper that had been at the cave, that meant an additional two men, the pilot and the two already here. Six against one.

Really bad odds.

Cord listened to Serna taunt him through a bullhorn or something like it. He couldn't see the chopper from his position, but from what he could hear he assumed they'd landed in the open field or lot just east of the visitor center.

"You are surprised to see me here, I think? Your friends, they were too late and did not find a thing. I have friends of my own. Just think, all this trouble could have been avoided if you had played along like your partner."

Sad, old ploy trying to get him to give away his position by shouting back a reply. Serna wanted him dead as much as he wanted Serna *taken care of.* He might be tired, but he'd never believe Shane was on Serna's payroll. *Now, how do I take this scum down without getting killed in the process?*

He'd made it to the parking lot without being seen. Thing was, he had no clue where Serna's men were. The snow wasn't his friend making his tracks visible on a moonless night. Serna must want him bad to force a pilot to risk flying in this soup. The snow was falling steady and might even ground that chopper for a while.

Excellent for him. Not good for Serna. Serna's pilot would be antsy to take off. Hanging around to kill Cord wouldn't be worth leaving that chopper for law enforcement to confiscate. Being in a hurry might cause mistakes, work to Cord's advantage.

"Are you waiting for a rescue? No one will come," Serna continued to taunt. "Your efforts are useless. Just give up and save us trouble."

Serna was attempting to distract him. Hard to do when he didn't have any plan to be distracted from. *Think!*

He wanted to walk up to Serna, defend himself and have it all done. If he really thought that would save Kate and their baby, he'd be willing to do it in a heartbeat. But Serna wasn't an honorable man. His vendetta was to make Cord suffer and the only way was to hurt Kate.

Don't think about her. Idiot. She's fine. She. Will. Stay. Safe.

You need to go Rambo on these guys. Cull them from the herd and take 'em out one by one. He heard her voice in his head. That concept was actually his only option. Separate. Disarm. Take them out one at a time.

Two minutes and he hadn't seen anyone near the car or on this side of the visitor center. It was worth checking out. His hot-wiring skills were rusty, but might be worth the effort. If not, he'd take the car out of commission, forcing Serna to leave in the chopper. And in this weather, that didn't give them a helluva lot of time.

No one was watching the car. He kept low, approached from the trees and lifted the handle. The door opened and he slid onto the seat. He popped the casing with his knife, dug for the wires and felt cold steel at his throat.

"You the bastard that shot me?" a shaky voice asked from behind him.

There had been three men in the car? Damn. "Is that a rhetorical question?"

"Hand me the knife and then the gun. You're lucky Jorje wants to kill you himself or I take pleasure slicing your throat."

"Yeah, real lucky." He flipped the knife around and, quicker than planning what to do, he plunged it into the fleshy part of the man's arm. Once. Then twice.

The threatening blade at his neck dropped onto his lap as the howl of pain from the backseat grew loud enough to wake the mountain.

IT WAS AMAZING how fast a tired, pregnant woman could climb another hill—even in a light snow—when her family was threatened. Kate ignored the soreness and shortness of breath. The air cooled her cheeks as she jogged to one of the highest peaks in the mountain range.

God, please let me get inside and call for help. And please keep Cord safe.

He's got to be safe. She heard Serna's voice echoing through the hills. As long as he was shouting for Cord to come out of the woods…she could only assume the madman didn't have him. Right?

If she could only go to the road and see if someone on duty had heard the helicopter or Serna's constant drivel. Warn them. Keep them from driving into Serna's thugs. Hopefully, whoever was in the observatory had already called the sheriff. Hopefully.

Her thighs on fire, she ached to stop with each step upward. She stepped on the high side of a small tree, put her hands on her knees and used the trunk to keep herself from falling backward. Wedging the butt of the rifle next to her for easy access, she wrapped the scarf tighter around her neck and covered her mouth, breathing the warmer air to keep her lungs from hurting as much.

A little flutter in her belly made her catch her breath. The baby moved. It gave her strength for the rest of the climb to the telescope. A powerful reminder to keep moving as fast as she could. Serna's yelling ceased and she stopped. She heard a light crunching of the snow. It could possibly be an animal scavenging for food. More likely, it was a two-legged animal hunting for her and Cord.

She stayed calm and brought the rifle to her hip. She couldn't see anything. Cloud cover and no moon equaled little visibility. What she had was blocked by the trees and darker patches next to them. She slowly raised the rifle to her shoulder. Ready.

Don't move. Steady. Aim. Don't hesitate. Cord can't rescue you this time.

Three or four trees over, she saw a puff of frosty breath. Then another. She waited. What was he waiting for? They wanted her alive!

Partner!

She turned just in time to see a body leap at her from her left. She pulled the trigger. The man stopped, his hands covering the wound in his stomach. In that split second she looked into his surprised eyes and saw the worry that his life was over.

Oh, my God!

She wanted to drop the rifle and help him. Didn't want him to die no matter what he'd done. Then that second was gone and she turned back around. The second man was running at her. Twenty feet. Fifteen. Ten.

The crazy-wild screams and curses let her know without a doubt that he had no intention of taking her back to

Serna. The knife raised high in the air would slice through her and the baby with little effort.

She didn't have enough time to raise the rifle. She swung the barrel in front of her and fired from her hip. The man took another step forward, pulling the knife back to his shoulder, ready to plunge into her when he was close enough.

Five feet.

She pulled the trigger.

THE REVERB FROM a second rifle shot echoed and faded, causing Cord to jerk as if he'd been the one hit. He couldn't let not knowing what had happened to Kate stop him or even slow him down. He couldn't allow himself to dwell on it.

After a couple of minutes of fighting, one whack with the back of his head had dazed the young kid long enough for Cord to completely subdue him. There were zip-tie handcuffs in the backseat—most likely to be used when they caught him. Now they were around the gang member, securing hands and feet to the floorboard seat frame.

"Ya gotsta help me, man. I bleed to death. You cut me bad."

"The gashes are deep, but I wrapped your jacket around the wound. If you don't move around, the bleeding will stop." He hoped. "So answer my question. Where did Serna move the drugs?"

"I don't know. I don't know."

"Then you're rather useless, aren't you?" He searched over his shoulder again, watching to see if this guy's partners were returning. He hated to do it, but he sliced and yanked electrical wiring under the dash to disable the car. Serna and his men couldn't use it to escape, but neither could he or Kate. Then he noticed what sat in the passenger seat, another fully loaded machine pistol. Thank God something was going right.

He had to find out what was going on. Serna had stopped jabbering. Two separate shots had been fired farther up the hill. Probably Kate since the gang members had been packing the automatics. A weapon he was now thankful to have in his hands. He closed the door, swung the strap of the pistol over his shoulder and ran to the north end of the parking lot. His only cover was the drainage ditch under the road where he'd intended for Kate to hide.

He ducked inside and crawled.

SWIPING THE FRUSTRATING tears that wouldn't stop, Kate had to admit that no one was inside working this particular telescope. The dome structure wasn't very large, but she'd walked around the entire thing twice, pounding on the outside with a rock.

She was so exhausted she couldn't imagine a level of tiredness above this. All she could think was that Cord was facing Serna alone and she couldn't do anything to help. There was no way to break inside. No car to borrow. She leaned against the door and slid to the ground. If she didn't stop crying soon, she'd end up with the hiccups.

"Idiot!" She'd come to the large telescope, but why would anyone be here on a night with so much cloud cover? Dormitories. "Where? Where? Where? There!"

She followed the path leading past a small brick building. Lights. She ran down the steps to the road. *Please, please, please be there.*

THE SLUSH SEEPED through his jeans and coat sleeves. Cord glanced at his watch as he crawled through the remainder of the pipe. It had only been twenty-two minutes. Just went to show how much could happen in a short time. He listened.

Nothing. Still no chatter from Serna.

Engines he hadn't noticed before. Chopper starting back

up? No, a car. But who? Too soon for the sheriff. Staffers. Had to be the staff checking out who had landed on their lawn. Took them long enough.

He ducked behind some tall grassy plant and searched for the remainder of Serna's men. Movement caught his eye. One of the men was playing sentry on the roof of the visitor center.

If he hadn't been cold before the wet had soaked through his clothes, the wind hitting him did it big-time. He waited until the man disappeared, then he stayed low and used the plants to block him from view. There was an opening at the bottom of the brick wall, and he crawled through. The headlights were closer, almost to the field. And plain as you please, two of Serna's men were waving their arms to get the car's occupants to see them.

Hostages.

What could he do? The sentry would take him out. He had no cover on either side of the brick wall. No buildings. No trees. Nothing. The car headed directly at the two men. All the driver would see was straps across their chests. The guns were hidden behind them and could easily be pulled forward.

"Damn."

Serna would use them to coax him out in the open by threatening to kill the driver. Even if the murderer didn't shoot him dead on the spot, he wouldn't need a hostage any longer and would kill them. Either way, the observatory staff would be dead.

The only choice left to him was to go out with a fight and take Serna with him.

Chapter Twenty

The headlights went off just before the curve at the top of the hill. The car stopped out of gun range, out of sight of the men standing in the field. Kate! She must be trying to come to his rescue and he couldn't allow that.

Very little cover in the open field. The only thing between him and that sentry/sniper was an evergreen at the corner of the building. Thin, but it might give him enough time. He needed to eliminate the threat closest to Kate first. Then the biggest threat of all—Serna.

Machine pistol on his back and knife in hand, Cord waited for the sniper to disappear to the far wall then ran toward the men. He had to disarm them both before they realized what happened. First and only priority—keep Kate safe.

He stayed as low to the ground as possible but couldn't stop to find out if the sentry sniper had seen him or not. No shots. He was in the clear until one of these yahoos yelled out. He dug deep for the energy to run. Drew on his training and memory to attack. He threw his shoulder into the back of the man nearest to him and kicked his legs to the side, knocking the second guy to the ground.

Neither of the men had their guns at the ready. Both started cursing and talking to each other in rapid Spanish. So rapid he couldn't keep up. It was clear the guy partially under him wanted help. Cord used the knife hilt on the back of his head, close to his neck. He stopped squirming.

One down, one to go.

The second man had rolled in the snow and was on his feet, weapon ready. Predictably, the man poked the barrel at him and when he did, Cord sliced his forearm. The man dropped the machine pistol and Cord body slammed him with everything he had left.

A shot hit the snow close to his left. Then another to his right. The sentry had seen the fight and drew a bead on him. Cord raised his hands behind his head, got to his knees and let the knife slide up his sleeve.

"Before you pull that trigger, I'm Cord McCrea. I think your boss wants to see me."

"Drop your gun."

Cord gestured that he needed to use his left hand, working the knife back into his palm.

"Slowly and carefully."

Cord pulled the strap over his head and watched the car back slowly the way it had come. He dropped the machine pistol and received a hard blow to the side of his head.

"On your feet. Now. Move." He pointed the barrel of the gun toward the chopper. "You are right, *amigo*. Serna wants to kill you himself and that pretty *chica* of yours."

Keep his attacker's mind off that car and keep Kate safe. No matter what—keep Kate safe. He wouldn't look to see where the car was, just kept working the hilt into his palm while he hid the action with his left wrist.

"Too bad. Kate's safe in the hands of U.S. Marshals by now," he said with a light shrug, faking that it mattered if the man believed him.

"That's for Jorje to think on. Get going."

Convince Serna that Kate wasn't with him. This minion hadn't seen her. Maybe it was possible. Then Serna would leave with the threat of the observatory staff calling the sheriff.

"Ah, Ranger McCrea," Serna tooted into the silence. "Bring him to the picnic area. Get the chopper ready, we can finally leave like you've wanted."

The slow whine of a chopper engine jerked his head away from the back of the visitor center where Serna waited for him. This was it. His only chance to stop the man who was terrorizing his family. One shot. Or blade.

Keep Kate safe. How? If they stayed here, she was at risk of being found. What if it wasn't her in the car? What if she was still in the trees, waiting for the right moment to take a shot. Then the sniper would take her out. He might be better than the last guy. His brain was taunting himself with the phrase "this is it" over and over again.

The shove in the middle of his back struck a sensitive nerve and made him stumble, but he managed to keep his hands in place behind his neck and the knife unseen. The trek to the picnic area was twice the length of a football field he used to run so easily and a lot farther to walk with a gun in his back.

He could use the blade on Serna if he could get close enough. But as the area where the drug lord was seated became clearer, there was a brick wall between them. His only option was to get Serna in close quarters and use the knife then. Get the enemy away from Kate.

He had time to slit the back of his jacket and get the knife inside the lining. Risky, slow, but he had the time. Deliberate movements, a few uncomfortable twists with his back to hide the drop. Now if they didn't make him leave his coat behind, he would be armed wherever they took him.

Of course, Serna could pull his gun and shoot him in the head. But, more likely, he'd enjoy beating him first. He'd want Kate's location, but Cord would never say. Besides, he didn't know and by the time he was asked it would definitely be the truth.

"This should be fun, I think," Serna said, walking toward him from the protection and warmth of the chopper.

Cord saw the left coming and braced his feet wider for the impact. Square in the jaw, the punch snapped his head to the side so fast he heard his neck crackle. Not only had he successfully stood his ground, he kept his hands behind his head instead of blocking or returning. The one to his gut put a catch in his breathing. But it was the hit from the rifle butt behind him that did the most damage.

He dropped to his knees in agony from the old back injury, the pain so fierce it made his head swim. Then a crack on his skull made it impossible to open his eyes. He could feel the blackness of unconsciousness taking hold of his senses.

Stay safe, Kate.

"What are you waiting for?" Kate screamed at the young co-ed she'd woken from a dead sleep. "Go. Go. Go!"

"But the helicopter's gone, ma'am."

"Do you think I'm going to wait here to be rescued? Drive me or get out. Every second I sit here he gets miles away."

"But the sheriff said to stay put and not move. We don't know who else is down there. They have guns."

"Can I borrow your car?"

"No. I'm driving back to the quarters and we're waiting."

The young woman put the car in Reverse and turned her little car around to head up the road again. Kate couldn't blame her. She doubted she'd believe the fantastical story of the past three days if she hadn't actually lived it.

Oh, my God, Cord, what did you do?

The young college student beside her had binoculars. Even in the low light she'd seen Cord run deliberately up to the two men in the field. He'd made a decision to get close to Serna. Probably trying to protect her. Not knowing for certain that she'd made the phone call to the Rangers, who should be headed this way in their own helicopter by now.

"May I borrow your phone again?"

The student handed her the cell from the seat next to her. "Sure, but it won't work until we get back to the house. Too many trees."

"Can you hurry?" She needed to call Cord's unit and tell them that Serna had one of their own. Maybe they could track him or something.

The woman—Kate couldn't remember her name at all—drove carefully through the snow. On a normal day, Kate would sit back and commend her for being so careful. Today was anything but ordinary.

Kate kept punching Redial even without the reception bars, hoping and praying the call would go through even seconds earlier. Her heart was racing and her palms were sweaty. And then a wave of dizziness hit her so hard she had to put her head back on the seat.

"Are you okay, Kate?"

"Just dizzy. I haven't had much to eat or drink today."

"I've got lots of food." The student parked the car in the bare spot she'd left pulling out earlier. "Sit there and I'll be around to help you inside."

Kate was past hungry, but knew she had to eat. But first, the phone was finally dialing.

"Sheriff Barber, this is Kate McCrea." She waited, her door was pulled open and she held up a finger, too afraid to move and lose the connection.

"Are you safe, Kate?"

"They left in the helicopter, flying southwest. They have Cord. It looked like they dragged him unconscious onto the seat and then took off."

"But are you safe?"

"Yes, or I wouldn't be calling you. Get someone tracking that helicopter. You've got to do something. Please. If anything happens to him, I don't— Oh God, he gave up. He did that to save me and all I did was watch."

"We're doing our best, Kate. Stay put and calm down. I'll contact the Rangers and see if they have any choppers available."

"How long?"

"I just passed the state park, sixteen miles away. Are any of Serna's men left?"

"I really don't know. I think so."

"Listen to me, Kate. Get inside, lock the doors and protect yourself. I'm at least twenty minutes out."

They disconnected and Kate was suddenly exhausted.

"The sheriff said to make certain everything's locked up tight. We don't know how many men were left behind." She accepted the help from the young woman to get inside the building. "What did you say your name was again?"

"I'm Sharon. Did your husband kill that guy? He fell to the ground and didn't get up. The guy from the roof ran to the helicopter just before it took off. Are you sure you're okay?"

There was no reason to correct her earlier mistake of calling Cord her husband. It was easier than explaining why her ex-husband was sacrificing so much to protect her. She'd convinced Sharon to drive her down the hill. It might take a long time to change how she thought about Cord.

"I'm just very tired and hungry." Kate turned the main light off. Leaning on the wall to close curtains, she looked around the room for the best spot to defend them.

"Hey, you better sit down. I can do all this." Sharon scooted one of the sofa chairs into the hallway, away from the windows and doors.

"I'm sorry you're in danger because of me." Kate could barely walk another step, but she made it and rested on a thick sofa arm. Her mind wouldn't stop. She could barely listen to what the young woman said about it being okay and probably saving her. Kate's head was imagining all the horrible things Serna would do to Cord. She was stuck on that flying death trap with him, sending all her energy, telling him to survive, praying and then praying again.

Out of the corner of her eye, she watched Sharon in the kitchen, chattering the entire time about normally loving her job. She accepted the cold sandwich while she waited on anyone to come through that door.

"Is the gun necessary?" Sharon eyed the rifle resting across Kate's lap.

One look and a nod of her head later, Kate fingered the safety off and waited. The sheriff had reminded her that Serna's men were still out there. She didn't know how many had come and didn't know how many would still be looking for her.

"I see headlights. The sheriff made great time. It's only been ten minutes."

"Get behind me, Sharon. Stay down and don't say a word."

Chapter Twenty-One

"Sharon?" a deep male voice shouted and he pounded on the door. "Sharon, are you in there? Open up."

"Kate," Sharon whispered, gently touching Kate's arm. "That's Logan. It's okay. He works here. I'm fine." She said the last words a bit louder so he could hear.

"Thank God. You wouldn't believe what we've been hearing over the scanner. Open up."

"You can put the rifle down, Kate," she said softly.

The young woman's hands covered Kate's grip, steadying the rifle that she'd pulled to her shoulder. They couldn't be sure who was out there. Someone might be forcing him. She understood that Sharon wanted her to set the rifle aside, but she couldn't. Not yet.

A louder banging on the door caused Kate to jump. "Tell him to go away. If he's really alone, he can go away."

Sharon ran to the window. "He's alone. It's okay."

"You don't know these men. They'll do anything. They could be holding someone else hostage."

"Sharon! Answer me or open this door."

The observatory employee nodded her head. "Logan, you need to drive out of sight. I'll call you when it's okay to come back. Don't ask why, just do it. I really am safe. I'll explain later."

Kate held firm. "No one but the sheriff is getting in that door."

"I understand. We'll wait together." She returned to her place behind Kate.

Kate tucked the fright in Sharon's voice away but she didn't care. Logan must have heard it, too. His car pulled away without another word. Right now, the rifle was staying in her hand and would stay pointed at the door until she knew it was safe. That was just the way it was. Period.

When the sheriff showed up a few minutes later, Kate finally slid the safety on but still held the rifle across her lap. Her elbow knocked the sandwich to the floor and Kate got on her knees to pick up the mess. That's where Sheriff Barber found her, crying.

She couldn't stop and knew the hiccups were going to take over soon. She'd make a fool of herself, sounding ridiculous, sobbing because a simple turkey sandwich covered the floor. She didn't care. She needed to cry. And cry. And then cry some more.

KATE WAS RIGHT back where she'd started two days ago. Wait. What day was it? She was wrong, it had just been the night before that she'd left with Cord. How could she have added an entire day? She really was tired.

Mrs. Burke opened the door, pulling her crocheted shawl around her shoulders for a little protection from the snow.

"I didn't know where else to take her, Juliet. She obviously needs rest and protection, but refused to stay at the observatory. Or go into protective custody. Said she wouldn't leave Valentine until we found McCrea. Maybe you can talk some sense into her."

Sheriff Barber was too young to have authority. She'd experienced so much more than this thirty-year-old Dallas ex-cop.

"I'm right here, Mike. Please stop talking like I'm not. And the last time I looked, I was a legal adult and didn't need anyone's permission to go anywhere. Nick," Kate said, looking at her friend and then his mother. "Juliet, I know this is a lot to ask. I understand it's dangerous to have me here. You can say no and I'll go to my ranch."

She spoke to Mrs. Burke, but Nick stood not two feet away. Arms crossed. Angry with each movement. Not saying a word. Typical man.

"Don't be ridiculous." Juliet wrapped her arm around Kate's shoulders and ushered her to the door. "You'll stay here until your father arrives."

The sheriff stepped across the porch toward Nick, securing his hat back on his head to protect it from the freezing air. Kate stayed in the doorway, listening, wanting to learn anything the authorities had refused to share with her, longing to fall asleep in Cord's arms and feel safe again.

"What are the chances he's still alive?" Nick asked.

"Slim," the sheriff whispered, and shook his head, his chin nearly dragging in defeat across his jacket. "I wish I could leave a deputy here, but we're all out searching. Mc-Crea's one of our own. We won't stop looking."

"He's alive, you know," Kate said from behind the screen, feeling the cold air rush into the warmth of the living room, but she couldn't close the door until they believed her.

Nick shifted from one leg to another. Nervous? Uneasy at her being at the house or overhearing? Or just uncomfortable at the thought she was holding on to a fantasy?

"Think about it," she explained. "Serna's had more than one opportunity to kill both Cord and me. But he didn't. Not in the years he was in prison and not by any of the men he's sent after us. This is a vendetta for him and he's vowed to make Cord suffer. There's no way he's killed him without getting to me." Her voice choked on the words and she pushed them out. "He'll make Cord watch."

"So you're agreeing that as long as you're alive, Cord's alive?" Nick asked, pulling the screen open to face her.

"I think so."

"Then get into protective custody. I can't protect you here, as much as I want to think I can." Nick pressed his lips together, shaking his head. "We don't have enough hands or guns to hold off the men Serna might have."

"He's right, dear." Juliet placed a comforting hand on her shoulder.

The sheriff stepped back onto the porch and held his hat in his hand, hypnotically smoothing the rim, turning the department-issued hat in a circle, over and over and over.

"Kate, Maddox is sending someone to pick you up. They aren't taking no for an answer and may very well force you into custody."

"Fine. I'll go. Can I at least have a bath and some of those fantastic eggs of yours, Juliet?" She couldn't argue with her only hope—if she was alive, so was Cord. So she needed to disappear. No local protective custody. Wherever she went she was putting someone in danger. So disappearing was the only option.

"Nick, help Kate to the guest room while I whip up some biscuits. Mike, you're staying until Kate's ride gets here, of course."

"If biscuits are involved, yes, ma'am." The sheriff nodded. "I'll keep an eye open. Holler when it's ready."

Kate turned to Nick. "I know where the guest room is. Go do whatever you're itching to do."

He ignored her suggestion and escorted her down the hall, following her inside the room so she couldn't close the door. "Are you really okay?"

"Yes."

"Mike said you were hysterical when he found you. That you wouldn't let go of the rifle."

"For a minute, but I'm fine. It's nothing that a couple of your mom's biscuits and a good, long sleep won't take care of." She hoped. Her hand rubbed her tummy. She could only pray nothing happened as a result of the past three days. "Really, Nick. I'm just very, very tired and I'm going to force myself to take a bath before I fall asleep standing here talking to you."

She forced herself to smile, attempting to reassure him that she believed what she was saying. It was half-true. Physically, she was just tired and needed food. Mentally though, well, worrying about Cord had never been this rough. It had been a "what if" game before. This was much too real and would follow them the rest of their lives—apart or together.

"I'm here if you need me. I always have been."

"I know and thanks."

"But?" he said with a twinge of disgust.

Definite attitude that she was too tired to deal with. "Look, we've been friends since elementary school. It's never been anything other than that, so what's the deal? I'm just too exhausted to tippy-toe around your ego."

He immediately backed out of the room with a hands-off gesture. "Got it. You're still in love with McCrea."

"So what if I am? He's my husband."

"*Ex*-husband."

She slammed the door in his face.

No matter what their marital status, Cord might very well be dead. Her child might grow up without her father. That scenario was completely unacceptable and there was nothing she could do about it.

Nothing except run away and hide. And that's exactly what Cord would want her to do. Stay alive. Protect their child.

"You ARE ONE lucky son of a bitch." He spoke low into the burner cell as soon as he could get out of earshot of all the people swarming the ranch. "She came back here to wait until they found McCrea."

"Bring her to me."

"It would be better if you ambushed their car when—"

"We're out of time. The buyers are impatient and we're ready to move."

"That's stupid. Three counties are covered with feds and state authorities trying to find you. They have special units covering the mountains. The state's bringing in more choppers."

"And they won't be looking for us to move the guns into Mexico. The diversion is necessary to make it across the border," Serna said, unusually calm. "We both know they're wasting their time in the mountains. We've moved to Danver's place just like we planned."

The level tone and pleasure exuding from the drug runner's voice gave him the creeps.

"You really are crazy. What if she'd gone home instead of here?"

"You agreed she'd never do that. If it had happened, you wouldn't have to get your hands dirty."

"Was this your plan all along?" He wondered if he was dealing with a madman or a cold, calculating, brilliant mind.

"You are too curious about details, *friend*. You might want to think hard on extending our partnership before we talk some more."

"I told you I'm out. That's always been the deal. The fire's a bit too close to home and the pan's getting awfully hot around here."

"You and your sayings. You have always amused me." Serna laughed. "I like having you around."

Those words were calculated. Innocent but a threat nonetheless.

For the first time since he'd begun dealing with these bastards, a chill ran down his spine. He shook it off. Showing fear wasn't the way to gain respect. And clearly telling them he wanted out was a death sentence. No matter what the understanding had been before, now wasn't the time to remind him. It was as plain as day he wouldn't be leaving alive if he took Kate Danver McCrea there.

"You know, Serna, I've only wanted one thing and you're about to take care of that. I'll have her at your *camp* soon and I'll think hard on reconsidering. Your operation is too smooth to just walk away. When I get there, we can decide the right amount of enticement to continue our arrangement."

Like hell he would. He was dropping her close to the gate and getting out of Dodge.

It was still his plan to become a witness for the government if he was caught. He had all the evidence safely tucked in a safe-deposit box. And if he wasn't caught…that island retirement looked better and better.

He laughed out loud. He just couldn't help it. Years of planning were finally paying off. Finally.

Chapter Twenty-Two

The smells were comforting, familiar. Cord knew them and relaxed. Couldn't place them for a couple of minutes until he took a deep breath—hay, manure, animals, leather. Barn. He drifted and woke with a start when a muscle in his shoulder cramped. Blasted shoulder. He must have slept wrong. He couldn't bring his hand around to work the muscle. Man, he was tired, and opening his eyes was difficult. Then he realized he was blindfolded, hands bound behind his back, face in the bottom of a stall.

No clue how long he'd been unconscious. He couldn't tell much of anything while he was blind as a bat.

This sealed it. Serna was working with a local rancher. Burke had been his first choice. But Cord wasn't gagged. Seemed to be out in plain sight, from the feel of the draft blowing across him. Serna's men wouldn't risk alerting Mrs. Burke and the hands. And every sense in him had to be totally skewed if Juliet Burke was a drug runner. No way. Where the hell was he?

His ribs were sore like he'd been kicked hard enough to bruise them. He licked his parched lips and could taste dried blood. He hadn't doubted Serna would kill him given the chance. Truth be told, when he'd let himself be taken by Serna's men he hadn't really thought further than keeping Kate and the baby safe.

Trying to get out of this mess alone wouldn't be easy, but he wasn't just giving up. He nudged his head against the ground. Slowly and painfully he inched the blindfold up so he could see and even blink. Still dark outside—at least that's what he could estimate from the nonexistent light. A dampness clung in the air from the snow outside and his muscles were stiff from the cold.

"Oh, man." His hoarse voice expressed his astonishment at recognizing the initials in the wood post of the stall. This was the Danver ranch. On their birthdays, David had notched both kids' heights into the first post, right-hand side, west door. He'd mucked this stall many times on his day off.

Serna had moved his operation here? How could the bold SOB know that no one was watching the place? It must have been Juan after all, but something more than the stall floor didn't smell right.

The door swung open, snow swirling inside along with a pair of fancy boots. No one working a ranch would wear slick dancing boots in this weather. Easy deduction that it was one of Serna's hirelings. He closed his eyes and nudged the bandanna mostly back into place. Better to play dead. Honestly, he could barely see straight, couldn't fill his lungs and had a stomach growling like a grizzly.

He could see enough to know the boots were next to him and he was about to be kicked to see if he was conscious. He prepared for the pain and would keep his body as silent as possible without tensing. Dear Lord, the pointed toe landed in his side in exactly in the same spot, with a force that might have just cracked the rib this time around.

He almost didn't breathe. In fact, he could easily have thrown up from the pain. *Think about Kate. That'll get you through it. Thinking about her got you through all the hard stuff last time.*

Kate was safe. She had to be. They wouldn't leave him

lying in a stall if they'd caught her. They'd be— *God, don't go there. You control the pain. The pain can't control you.*

He remained motionless several seconds after he heard the boots shuffle out and the bounce of the wooden latch fall into place. The desire to curl into a ball might have prevailed if his hands had been at his stomach. He couldn't take another of those kicks. Boots-man might just puncture a lung next time. Then where would he be?

Zip-tie handcuffs.

Knife. He hadn't searched to see if his knife was still in the lining of his jacket.

The secured circles of hard plastic bit into his skin and made it harder to bend his hands to search the bottom of his jacket. The pocketknife had moved around the lining but it was workable. Getting it open wasn't as difficult as fighting the burns the plastic biting his wrists caused.

Slow. Steady. He worked the blade open, cut easily enough through his coat—okay, David's coat—and got the blade into his hand. Cord was determined to saw the cuffs in half and free himself. He knew all about determination. His stubbornness kept his legs moving as he learned to walk and then run again. He had controlled the pain for two years of intense therapy. He'd control the pain now.

And when he found Boots-man, he'd make sure there was some kicking involved and not to his ribs. He manipulated the blade using his watchband for a little leverage and protection. Lying on his side, his arms just wouldn't move back and forth enough to break through the stinking plastic.

He had to risk sitting and was fortunate they hadn't taken the time to secure his feet. With his head swimming, he pushed himself up and rested against the slats separating the stalls. At least he wasn't as cold anymore. He positioned the knife again and began the tedious back and forth sawing motion necessary to escape.

A LIGHT KNOCK on the door woke her. Just flipping the afghan off made her body scream to stay put and not move for a week. She rubbed her eyes, looking for the alarm clock across the room. Midnight and still snowing.

"Yes?"

"May I come in?"

"Sure, Nick."

He brought her a second tray with a teapot, biscuits and honey. The one before her nap had been a little bit of heaven. Then an image of Cord filled her mind. Shot, bleeding, unable to walk and passing out as she screamed at him. She covered her eyes, trying to focus on anything at all, only to see it even more clearly.

If he can survive that, he can do this. He will survive. He has to survive. Her hands dropped protectively over their baby.

"Hope you don't mind the interruption. Mom thought it important to get some more food and tea down you." He set the bed tray across her legs and crossed to the window.

"Thanks." She could tell he wanted to say something to her. It was just like the time he asked her to the homecoming dance even when he wanted to go deer hunting. Some habits never changed. "How does the weather look and what's the latest estimate on my ride out of here?"

"Not good and getting worse on the snow. They're predicting three or four inches by morning. Choppers are grounded." He stuck his hands deep into his jeans pockets. "Mike left a couple of hours ago, before we knew there may be a problem with help coming in from Pecos."

"You're worried. I'm sorry. Your mom and dad are here and I'm putting them in danger. I should have thought things through."

"We're family. You should come to us. I just don't know

how effective I'll be with the few rounds I have left. I'm assuming Cord's the one who took my ammo."

"So he wiped you out?"

"Pretty much, yeah. Glad I thought to check when the
sheriff left."

"So you'll drive me into Marfa or Fort Davis?" Why
wouldn't he look at her? Had they heard something else? If
they had, he would have told her first thing. No, this was to
do with Nick himself.

"I feel like I'm letting you down."

That was the crux. "It's my fault, Nick. I should have
thought about this before I demanded the sheriff bring me
here. You're the one who convinced me to reconsider. You
haven't let me down and I'm sorry I slammed the door in
your face earlier." She hugged him and received one back.
"I'll have my shoes on and be out the door in ten minutes."

"I'll warm up the car."

It was nice knowing she wouldn't have to worry about
mending fences in this weather. But she'd miss her friends.
The relief only lasted until she opened the door. The wind
and swirling snow hit her square in the face and a chill
spread through her body. Where was Cord? Was he out of
the snow and north wind? Was he even alive?

Kate ran down the path to the waiting car. She hoped the
car warmed up fast. Its exhaust formed a white cloud from
the tailpipe, but the windows were still frosted. Odd. Why
hadn't Nick scrapped the windows clean? The little instinct
that raised the hairs on the back of her neck kicked into high
gear. Her steps slowed and she stopped altogether when the
driver's door opened on the far side of the car.

"Oh, Mac. You sort of scared me. I was expecting Nick
to drive me." She pulled the handle to open the door.

"There's a problem with a mare he's been keeping an eye

n and he asked me to drive you. Do you feel safe enough
vith an old man?"

She pulled the door open and immediately saw the blood
patter. She pivoted to run, but the click of a gun readying
o fire stopped her in her tracks.

"I should have said, you shouldn't feel safe with this old
nan. Get in."

"Is he dead?"

"Nick?" He put the car in gear and bounced them down
he road. "Frankly, I didn't check and don't care."

The duffel from the lodge was in the backseat floorboard.
o the drugs were Mac's and he'd been hiding them. Mac
`auldwell was a family friend. Someone she'd trusted. And
e was the "ranch owner" Cord was certain existed.

"How much is Serna paying you?"

"A lot." He turned the corner a bit fast and the back of
he car fishtailed. He laughed widely. "It's enough to finally
et out of this desert and retire in comfort."

The wild-eyed look in Mac's eyes scared her into silence.
hree years ago, he'd known she and Cord would be at the
inch for dinner. "Why are you working with these horrible
onsters? What did we ever do to you?"

"It's all the more fun because you think there has to be
reason." His laughter grew; he was almost tearing up he
as hee-hawing so much.

"You're laughing at causing my family so much pain?
ou're responsible for everything. You knew we'd be at
ad's that night. You killed my baby girl."

"Naw. All I did was tell Serna where'd you be."

"If you hadn't given the drug cartel access and details to
ir land, none of this would have happened."

It was tempting to reach out and grab the wheel, send
em careening into the barbed-wire fence. Or to reach for
e gun he casually held in his hand now. Mac might refer

to himself as old, but he was still a sinewy cowboy. She
seen him wrestle a cow to the ground last summer and wi
the senior division with the best time. Because of the bab
she couldn't risk a car wreck or gunshot wound. All sh
could do was hope for a last-minute miracle.

"Nothing would have happened? I wouldn't be too su
of that, missy. If it hadn't been me, Serna would have four
someone else. There are plenty of people on his payroll. Ju
'cause I'm helping this time around doesn't mean anythin
will be different when I leave. Just that someone else wi
be helping." He turned onto the drive to her house.

"What are we doing here?"

"The final joke's on you." He threw back his head laug
ing, hitting the window with the gun. "While everyone
searching for Serna and that precious Ranger of yours
the mountains, he's been running up the heating bill in yo
house. Probably sleeping in your bed. But you won't have
worry about that for long. Take off your shoes."

"But it's snowing."

"Yeah, I got that. Now take 'em off." The laughter disa
peared from his craggy, thin face. "I'm not sticking arou
to let Serna get the best of me. I'm out of here."

She bent her knee and frantically unlaced her boot, ho
ing he wouldn't see the string she wadded up within her fi
She got both laces down the back of her jeans before he g
to the last cattle guard.

They stopped. "Get out."

"Are you going to shoot me? I thought Serna wanted
do that."

"I don't know what he'll do and I don't care. But wh
ever happens, I'll be long gone or making a deal for witne
protection. As long as I get my cut, I'm good. Now get ou

She scooped up her shoes and pushed open the door.
reached across and knocked the shoes into the floorboa

"Nope. These stay. Nowhere to run this time, missy. You're pregnant and barefoot and Serna will be here any minute. Hasta la vista." He shoved her out of the Jeep.

She landed hands, knees and freezing toes in six inches of snow. He gunned the engine and she crawled out of the way just before he turned and headed back the way they'd come. The icy wetness seeped through her cloth gloves and pants. She didn't want to stand, but did. The snow was cold and didn't take long to start stinging her feet.

"Now what do I do?"

She saw the familiar sight of her home about a mile away. There was nothing else around and her feet quickly screamed the only available option.

Walk home. Straight into the grasp of the devil.

Chapter Twenty-Three

Cord jerked awake from a long fall in his dream. No wonder, since he was perched, hiding in a vee of the barn rafter.
Another doze starting with thoughts of Kate and ending wi
the inability to protect her. Back to finding a way to sto
Serna. Missing Kate didn't have any place in his thought
but it was there nonetheless.

He stretched a bit and used his right index finger to g
his wedding ring from the change pocket of his borrowe
pants. The silver band slid onto his cold finger as easily
the first time. His hand felt wrong without it. They'd bee
divorced on paper for a little over five months, but he
never been able to leave it on his dresser more than a co
ple of days.

Actually, divorced wasn't the same as feeling divorce
He'd seen Kate at the fence and his first thought was to ki
her hello. Same thing had happened the night before the
court date. Only then, he'd kissed her. And then a lot mor

Man, he was going to miss her. Every day and a lot of n
nights he'd be thinking about her and the baby. He'd total
screwed up and there was no way out now.

She had to be in protective custody by the sheriff, ma
shals, Rangers—some organization that would keep h
safe. Truth be told, he couldn't. He'd be lucky to keep hi
self alive through the night.

He had two options to get inside the house and to Serna—surprise the next one through the door and call for backup with the man's cell, like he'd been waiting in the barn rafters to do for a while now. Or wait for his escape to be discovered and sneak into the house. So far it was the first option.

While he'd been looking for a weapon, he'd raided the barn mini fridge Frank had in his office. With the setbacks Cord had caused Serna in the past several days—losing at least nine men—the criminal still seemed more arrogant than ever. No one had bothered to look in on him for at least forty-five minutes.

What the heck are they waiting on?

"Kate."

No one had left the ranch—he would have seen or heard a vehicle. That left the rancher who was working with Serna. That scum had to be delivering Kate to her very own front door. They weren't worried about Cord waking up, assuming he was less of a problem unconscious.

He couldn't wait here any longer. He had to act now. He swung down from his hidden perch in the corner. He'd thought about what to do when Kate's words came back. *"Can't you go Rambo on them or something?"*

Armed with only a pocketknife, a pair of hay tongs and the cover of darkness, he climbed from the spot where he'd waited. Since no one had come for him, it was time to take the fight to his enemy one by stinking one.

"Cull them from the herd and take 'em out one by one." Kate had told him exactly what he needed to do. He took off his jacket. There would be plenty of activity to keep him warm and the bulky coat would only hinder his fighting. He'd already cut the fingertips from his gloves so he'd have a better grip.

"Okay, babe, the threat on you ends tonight," he whispered into the darkness. He slipped out the door, away from the house. It faced nothing but the dark corral and snow-covered pasture. With no one in sight, he stayed close to the wall, breathing through his nose, limiting the puffs of frost in front of his face.

He'd heard the sentry earlier, someone walking the perimeter of the barn but doing a sloppy job of it in the cold. He stayed at the edge of the corner, waiting. Far sounds. No chatter. He slid along the next wall, hidden in the shadows, pausing again at the corner until he heard the snow crunch. He drew his palm back, ready to strike. One solid, unexpected blow to the man's face and he was done. Silent, with the thudding exception of the falling body. Serna's force was now one less.

Taking the man's hat, jacket and weapon, he walked around the corral and barn as if he were the man he'd just left in the snow. Serna's men seemed to have an endless supply of machine pistols. Cord hated to think that he'd been out of the investigation so long he didn't know if this was the real cargo coming across the border.

He wanted to take more than just one of Serna's men down before approaching the house and confronting the man in charge. But he had to find them first. The far side of the ranch buildings had a yellow glow next to the field. As he approached, the noise level grew. The sound of men hustling and issuing orders, pounding feet. They were moving cargo from or into a semitrailer.

Damn. They'd moved their operation here to Kate's ranch. The idea of her family being desecrated gave him a lump in his throat. The ranch was the reason she'd refused to leave town for so long, even after they'd been threatened the first time by Serna.

The men leaving the truck were empty-handed. The driver started the rig, warming the diesel in preparation to leave. Whatever they were doing, they were almost finished.

and getting ready to pull out. They wouldn't risk a semi packed with drugs. It didn't make sense. They'd break up heroin shipments, not put it all in one location. Too risky if they were pulled over. The men he watched didn't seem in a hurry, so moving everything in one shipment wasn't because they were afraid of being caught.

The last men dropped off their box and walked away from the truck. The lights went off and he heard the whine of a chopper starting, finding it on the other side of the men. He needed to get a look at what was inside the trailer to know how to deal with it. Or did he? That was the Ranger in him...the part constantly seeking the answer to the confounded questions of how Serna was accomplishing everything. Cord, the husband and father, only needed to get rid of those men and call for backup.

He picked his way around the edge of light, staying hidden. He'd counted six men warming around a fire they'd started on the ground. That meant six ways to cull each of them from the equation. Or something that would distract several.

Fire. Fire rushing toward the chopper and the truck might occupy all of them long enough to find Serna. He needed the gas Danver stored near the toolshed.

"He has to be around here somewhere."

"I saw a man wearing Edward's hat by the truck. He should be guarding the barn."

Cord darted inside the small building, just behind the door to determine how many men were outside. He raised the hay tongs, waiting.

One man stuck his head inside the shed and Cord swung the metal, catching him across his face. He dropped to the ground but not before the second man opened fire into the shed. Cord rolled to his back and pulled the trigger of his weapon, not aiming, just shooting in an arc through the open door. One shot after rapid shot.

The return fire ended and he heard a hard thump hit the ground. Cord recognized the man he'd knocked in the nose. "Hello, Juan." He dragged the unconscious slime inside the shed, calf-roping his hands and feet. "Guess that explains how they knew no one was here at the ranch. But if you're here, who's bringing Kate?"

Sliding in the snow, he rounded the corner, opened the top of the gas drum and turned it on its side. The gas splashed to the earth. All he needed was a lighter and those men would be occupied trying to save their unknown cargo in those crates.

CONFUSED AT MAC'S BETRAYAL, Kate continued the difficult walk through her property. She'd quickly realized who and what was waiting inside her home. Serna. It hadn't fully sunk in that Mac was involved with drug smugglers. She'd known the man her entire life. It was almost like having an uncle betray her family.

As Kate drew near the house, she noticed the rifle barrel. Her feet were on fire from being so cold even after she'd laced her wet gloves to the bottom of her socks for a little protection. The bits of string had come in handy after all.

The man pointing the gun in her face knocked on the front door. Serna came through, wiping the corner of his mouth with one of her mother's lace napkins from the antique buffet.

Bastard.

"Time to leave. When will the helicopter be ready?" The murderer ignored Kate.

The man shrugged. "Till it's deiced. Safe or crash. Your choice."

She thought Serna would strike him, but the man walked

off toward the east pasture. She'd never felt an emotion as powerful as the hatred she had for the man responsible for her child's death. It was horrible and would consume her if she weren't careful. She had to control the rage. Harness it into energy she needed to help Cord with their escape.

COME ON, MAN. Cord patted the pockets of the coat. Nothing. The cab of the truck was right there. He found a lighter and killed the ignition, taking the keys with him. It would defeat the purpose of lighting everything up like a roman candle if they could just drive away.

Back in the shadows, he got close to the truck and shoved the barrel with all his strength. A trail of diesel melted a path in the fresh snow.

Lighter. Flame. Toss. Fire. Run.

Wait for it....

SHE AND CORD would escape. There was no way they could let this evil man win whatever game he was playing. Kate wanted to claw Serna's eyes out, but the handgun in the front of his pants prevented her. If given the chance, she knew where the weapons were stored. There was a loaded gun locked in its safe in her bedside table that opened with her thumbprint, a gift from her husband.

"It's been a long chase, Kate McCrea. You got a nice place here."

Serna attempted to sound at ease and maybe a little more cultured than usual as he led the way through the kitchen. But it didn't make him anything better than the filth she scraped from the bathtub drain.

"Sit. Warm up a bit."

He'd definitely made use of her house. A kitchen chair was waiting in front of a huge fire. She sat while Serna reclined in her father's lounger with a half-eaten steak on the end table. He'd just taken a bite when the door slammed open and a short young man burst in.

"He ain't there, boss."

"Find him!" Serna shouted. He threw his plate and hit the retreating messenger. Continuing his Spanish curses, he paced the room, then peered out the window and yanked the blinds. Their crash to the floor made her flinch inside and out.

The long-bladed knife he used to slice the cord appeared from nowhere. He wrapped the cord menacingly around his fist. The evil in his glaring intent made her shiver and want to run to save herself.

"Find him!" The shouts from outside continued as Serna advanced.

The muscles in his clenched jaw twitched. He was worried. Then it sank in who they were searching for.

Cord was gone from wherever they'd been holding him. That was suddenly clear. She fought the upturn of her lips, but not the pride filling her heart.

Men began yelling *blanket* in Spanish. Something had gone wrong. At first she thought the fire was reflected in the window, but it was outside, somewhere on the other side of the barn and spreading. Quickly.

An explosion split the silence, flames shot into the sky ridding the night of the frightening darkness for a moment. The force shook the walls of the house. The vibration burst through her thawing feet. Something big and close to the shed. Maybe the tractor fuel?

"McCrea!" Serna screamed into the window.

She was ready to run, and ready to react to however this monster came after her. She picked her route through the house. The front hallway to the bedroom and the gun box. If he followed…pull the trigger.

Chapter Twenty-Four

The force of the gas explosion dropped him to his knees. He'd almost made it to the back of the shed when the hot blast of air knocked him to the ground. He sat on his butt in what used to be darkness, watching shards of the barrel burning around the field, then scurried backward until he hit the fence. Serna's men ran to the semi using their jackets to put out the flame. At this rate, they'd be successful in a matter of minutes.

On the other side of the fire, the chopper blades were still at slow speed. Cord watched the pilot open and shut the door. He tightened his grip on the machine pistol. Too far to shoot. But the semi keys were still in his fist.

He ran the perimeter shadow. The driver was in the cab searching for keys. Cord caught him across his shoulder blades on his way down. Another bad guy sprawled in the snow. To keep the truck in gear and get clear, his lone option was to shove his machine pistol against the gas pedal. It was the only way to put both the truck and the chopper out of commission. He'd pick up the driver's gun on the way back.

Cord cranked the semi, shoved it into Reverse, not caring what was in his way. If there were drugs in the back of this thing, the horses and cattle might be high for miles. He wedged the pistol into place and jumped from the truck cab.

Men began yelling. Jumping out of the way. Running. Cord got to the downed driver just as the truck backed through the major fire. It didn't stop and caught the tail rotor of the chopper as it lifted off.

The crash sent the chopper spinning into the field. It tipped, the blades digging into the ground, sending the body end over end. Time to move. The driver had a machine pistol that Cord jerked from his body. He moaned and Cord flipped him to his back, sticking the barrel in his face.

"Up."

The man staggered to his feet and Cord shoved him to the shed and roped his hands and feet behind his back like a steer. He stuffed work rags into both men's mouths to keep them quiet.

Cord draped a second gun over his shoulder and searched their pockets. Cell phone. The Sheriff's department answered on the first ring.

"This is Cord McCrea, I'm located at the Danver ranch. There's been an explosion and I need backup."

"Cord, thank God you're alive. We have every available person searching the mountains. I'll reroute everyone and send a fire truck. Wait for reinforcements. There's a chopper at the observatory that can be there in ten."

"Can't wait. Serna moved his operation. Come in hot. I'm uncertain about the number of guns. Gotta go."

"Cord, Nick Burke was shot and we think—"

The devil could take Burke if he'd been working with Serna and received his comeuppance. He cut off the call since he didn't want to be talked out of his plan to eliminate Serna and the threat to his family. A lot could happen in ten minutes—if reinforcements could actually arrive by then.

Cord was willing to accept the consequences of all his actions.

THE BLOOD VESSELS in the side of Serna's neck were visibly enlarged. He was enraged about the explosion and Kate no longer knew if he'd wait until Cord was there to hurt her. She had to get to the gun.

Was an all-out run better than inching her way to the hall? She had socks—actually, knit gloves—on her feet. With no shoes on the wooden floors and stinging prickles making her feet ache, running would be a disaster. She remained in the chair. As soon as she stood, he'd know her intention. She slid a foot closer to the fireplace tools, a weapon, something to give her a fighting chance.

What would Cord do? He'd give himself two ways out. So she curled her legs to each side of the chair and quickly pushed her socks down around her ankles. She'd time her movements to get the slick cloth off her feet. If she couldn't get shoes from her bedroom, she had a set of mud boots in the barn.

Success, one bare foot.

Serna hit the wall with both fists, then spun around to face her. She met his crazy-eyed stare and wouldn't look away. Fear of what an insane person filled with revenge would do ended up giving her strength to meet him straight on. If she made a move, she was three or four feet away from the fire tools.

Her enemy's face was the color of the bloodred middle oozing from his T-bone. His hands were still at his sides, not close to the butt of the gun. She didn't have enough time to grab the shovel or poker without his drawing and shooting her in the back. He wouldn't miss. Not this time.

Enraged as he was, he wasn't ranting around the room like three years ago. And this time, she was much more frightened. She couldn't see a way out. Armed only with shoelaces? What had she been thinking?

"Your husband has made my life hell." He cocked his

head like a curious dog. "What, no response? Aren't you going to beg for your life?"

"Would it do any good?" Second sock at her toes.

"No."

"Then I'll just wait."

"Wait for the end?" He caressed the clip of his gun wedged down the front of his pants.

She choked back a laugh at the thought of him shooting himself in the crotch and ending this nightmare. She must be very tired to let her imagination venture down that road.

"You find it funny? McCrea can't rescue you. Not here."

"No." There was movement outside the window. Cord? Serna caught the direction of her eyes and began to turn. "Well, yes, actually I find it hilarious." He pivoted back to her. "After all your work, an explosion is going to bring people from miles around. But I imagine you don't find that funny at all."

"No time for games." He removed the gun and aimed it at her. The string from the blinds was dangling from his hand. "Stand up and turn around. We're leaving."

She stood, barefoot, ready to run.

Serna jerked her hands behind her, wrists on top of each other and tied. She didn't move but frantically searched the windows and mirrors trying to find a glimpse of Cord

Gun in his right hand and his left holding her bound wrists, he shoved her toward the front door.

What would Cord do? He'd be waiting just outside that door.

Serna opened the door and pushed her into the screen She pretended to stumble, bending her body almost in half just in case her rescue was about to begin.

"Get up!" Serna yelled, jabbing her with the gun.

A jet stream shot above her head, aiming toward Serna'

face. She was shoved forward by Cord. He stepped between her and Serna's gun just as it went off.

"No!" She fell to the front porch, rolling to her back, using her feet to slide out of the way.

Cord wasn't shot. He pushed inside, jabbing something into Serna's chest. "Get out of here, Kate."

The machine gun bounced on the floor and the men used their fists on each other too fast for her to count the blows. The screen was still propped open by her feet. She scooted, stood, got back inside.

Her gun. She ran, opened her nightstand. She heard another weapon fire from the living room. She was certain her pistol was loaded. It would be so much easier to have her hands free. No time to find a kitchen knife. She heard the click after placing her thumb in the scanner. She grabbed the pistol and ran back to the living room.

The men were rolling, punching, grunting. Serna still had his weapon. There was blood on Cord's side, across his face. Both of his hands were holding Serna's in place away from him.

With her hands behind her back she couldn't help or use her own pistol. Serna's strength seemed to be prevailing. He was lying across Cord, pinning his legs. They seemed to be deadlocked—both gripping each other's wrists. A contest of sheer willpower. She could see the determination on Serna's face and the desperation on Cord's.

"Run," Cord demanded.

She couldn't run, she had to help. This was their fight, not just Cord's job. She dropped the gun on the floor close to Cord's head. She ran to the hearth and picked up the fireplace tools. She couldn't wield anything backward, but she could drop it all onto Serna's back.

Close to both men again, Serna guessed her intention and rolled off Cord, knocking her feet from under her. She fell, unable to avoid colliding with the brick hearth. Trying to absorb the impact to her midsection, she heard the discharge.

"Are you okay?" Cord asked.

She opened her eyes, saw her gun in his hands and Serna on his back, unmoving across her father's footstool.

"Yes," she answered, still trying to catch her breath. A tight pinch started in her back and quickly spread across her abdomen. "Oh, God, Cord, what have I done? I think I'm in labor."

He was by her side in an instance. "I'm here, babe. We've got this."

Chapter Twenty-Five

"We're almost there. Just hold on." Cord steered the old Ford past the city limits sign, very familiar with the route to the county hospital.

"She's only five months, Cord. She can't be born this early. What if—"

"No 'what ifs.' They'll give you something. Contractions will stop. You'll be fine. Just try to relax. Maybe that will help." He swerved back into his lane, glad no one else was on the road to Marfa during a snowstorm in the middle of the night. "Go ahead, say it."

"The contractions are about fifteen minutes apart. You're right, I just need to relax. We'll be there soon enough if you can stay on the road." She laughed, smiling at him in the rearview mirror. "But it is hard to relax thinking we'll be headed into the next gully."

He slowed and it hit him how much pain and worry he'd caused her during their time together. It would be a miracle if she ever forgave him.

"Kate, I...I'm sorry. Whatever happens, this has all been my fault and I'm sorry."

She sighed and wrinkled her forehead for a serious look. "For the record, I blame Jorje Serna, one hundred percent. Not you. I've never blamed you."

He blamed himself and would continue to blame himself.

The last time he'd come through the E.R. doors, he'd been on a gurney, fading in and out of consciousness. At least this time he ran inside after slamming the car into Park, blocking access to the automatic doors, and began looking for familiar faces. Familiar or not, he latched on to the first person in scrubs he found and started dragging them to the door.

"Kate's in the car, five months' pregnant, contractions approximately fifteen minutes apart. The last one was about seven minutes ago."

The nurse or E.R. worker resisted and he grabbed a wheelchair and went to get his wife himself.

"Wait, Cord! We'll get her."

He heard them shouting but that wouldn't stop him. They couldn't lose this baby. They just couldn't.

Kate had gotten out of the car, holding her small tummy. It wasn't the normal E.R. pregnancy picture an expectant father wanted to see. He wanted to see her belly grow. He wanted to experience every part of life with her. Not apart.

"Good, you got a chair." The relaxed calmness evaporated as she reached out to spread his shirt wide and look at the bloodstain. "Oh, my God, Cord. Were you shot?"

He covered his side, remembering the sting he'd felt at the front door. "Must be from someone else."

"You're a horrible liar," she said, and sat in the chair for him to wheel her through the doors. "Would you please take care of Cord? He's been shot again."

Kate had stopped the first nurse who'd come to take charge of the wheelchair, flashed them a smile, a thank-you and acted as if they weren't in the fight of their lives.

Cord had a flash of that night three years ago. Maybe it was a memory or just his imagination, but the anxiety currently thrumming through his system was worse than wondering where the next shot was coming from. He could return fire, defend himself, anticipate what might happen.

Here, in this hospital, he didn't have much more than the feeling of hopelessness. He'd lost everything here and each day he'd awoken here, each time he'd returned for a doctor's appointment, he'd been reminded of how much he'd lost.

He stood five feet away from Kate, refusing to move to the next curtained area. Dumbfounded? In shock? He couldn't tell. He sort of watched things happen around him and thought about everything as it did. Doctors and nurses moved around him. Someone took him by the shoulders and said, "At least stay at the head of the bed so we can work."

Needles, IV bags, monitors and voices that didn't completely register. Dozens of people helped her and he just stood there. Unable to react or help her. It was out of his control.

Was he losing it?

He'd never been an emotional man. When he said something, he meant it and he'd always assumed the person listening knew he meant it. Kate knew, didn't she? Knew that he loved her more than life?

How often did you tell her? He heard the shrink's question. And his answer had been "all the time." But had he?

"I love you, Kathleen."

Motion in the room stopped.

"I love you, too, Cord. Now will someone check under all that blood? I'm telling you, the man has been shot."

"Not shot, just cut, I think," Cord clarified for her.

They began working again and a doctor he'd never met— he knew plenty of them at this place—lifted his shirt and mumbled a curse.

"Someone get this man a bed," the doctor said.

"I'm not leaving. Do whatever you have to do, but I'm staying by her side as long as she needs me." He looked in Kate's eyes and knew she understood the full meaning of his words. He'd go wherever she needed him to. Give up anything for her. There'd be plenty of time to decide what they were doing once this baby was safe.

He also saw her love. It shot through him, energizing more than the physical part of him. She gave him the strength to conquer whatever life threw at him.

"We're getting married," he announced to the nurse squirting a stinging solution on his side.

"There he goes again," Kate said, smiling in spite of their uncertain future, "making plans without ever asking me the question."

"Is there a question to ask?"

She shook her head. "Just say when and where."

Epilogue

"Did Mr. Cauldwell tell you why he gave you a ride to your ranch?" Mac's attorney asked.

"No, he did not. And it wasn't a 'ride,'" Kate stated under oath.

It had been four months of secretive living, overprotection and major bed rest. Kate had fought the doctors about returning for the grand jury hearing. Once Mac had been apprehended, the prosecuting attorneys had pushed to get her testimony on record while she was still pregnant. "More effective and personal."

Right. She was as big as a house and her back was killing her because of the hours on a wooden chair across the hall.

"Did Mr. Cauldwell ever state that he'd shot Nick Burke?"

"Not in those words, no." Kate hated to admit he hadn't confessed and avoided looking in the direction of where Mac sat.

"So it's possible you could have misunderstood what he'd said. And it's possible he'd received instructions from his boss, Nick Burke, to drop you at your home?"

"He drove off with my boots." She pointed to an evidence bag at the side of the room. They'd been found along the ranch's drive near the main road. "He said Serna would be there to pick me up. And let's be perfectly clear, Mac knew

I was pregnant and knew that monster intended to kill me, not buy me new shoes."

A low amount of laughter rippled through the room. Kate smiled until a contraction tightened her belly even tighter than the stretched-to-capacity skin. She looked at Cord, who hadn't looked away since they'd walked in.

"Just answer the question put before you."

"Kate?" Cord stood, hands on the railing separating him from the back of the prosecutor.

"Sit down, Mr. McCrea," the judge instructed.

"I'm fine." She smiled at her husband. "Really." Cord sat but stayed on the edge of the long bench, his knuckles turning white against the dark stain of the railing.

Mac still had a smile on his face as if he seriously didn't care what she said. That it didn't matter. But this trial would determine if he went into witness protection or if he spent the rest of his sorry life behind bars.

It was the only reason Cord had finally conceded to returning to Texas for the trial. They had talked, discussed, weighed the pros and cons. Ultimately, he agreed he wanted Mac to pay for his crimes, not walk free.

"Again, Mrs. McCrea, is there a possibility that the defendant had misunderstood instructions from his employer?"

He would not walk free. She waited until the man who had betrayed her family looked at her. Waited longer while the constant smile changed to a worried frown. "There is no way Mac Cauldwell misunderstood anyone. He dropped me a mile from my home, shoeless with snow on the ground. He knew what he was doing and he stated that he didn't care."

Another contraction, much too soon after the first, made her pause long enough for the defense attorney to whine.

But as soon as she could breathe again, she continued what she needed to say to keep Mac behind bars.

"He admitted that if he got caught he had evidence that would put him in WitSec. This man has no regard for the loss of life or horrible things he's done. He deserves to rot in prison, not be rewarded with a new life."

"Kate, you're going to have to restrict— Are you okay?" the judge asked.

"Sorry, but I—" She could barely talk while the contraction subsided. "I think I'm in labor."

THREE POLICE CARS pulled into the Alpine hospital, escorting them to the emergency entrance. They were greeted at the door with a wheelchair and the doctor Kate had seen for the first half of her pregnancy. And yet, Cord had never been so frightened in his life. He'd just thought he'd been afraid. What if something happened to Kate? She was high risk after the past four years. Something could go wrong.

"Welcome back, Kate. Doing okay?" the doctor asked.

Kate panted, obviously in the middle of another contraction.

Cord looked at his watch. "That's less than two minutes since the last one."

"I think we should have us a baby," the doctor told Kate, who nodded in agreement.

Kate laced her fingers through his as she was wheeled straight to the maternity wing. He stood in a corner out of the way, continually turning down the offer to sit in the chair or move to the waiting area. He would be by Kate's side the entire time no matter how useless he felt. Guns he could handle. Horses he could work in his sleep. But worrying about Kate was a full-time job.

"Cord," Kate called, waving him closer. "You look like you're about to throw up. Are you okay?"

The doctor entered the room and proceeded to do her thing checking on Kate. Truth be told, he didn't know how he felt. He was about to be a father.

"Well, Kate. Things are progressing nicely and it probably won't be too long. I'll be back when I'm needed."

They were alone, something that would have scared him to death five months ago, but he loved it now. He'd spent a lot of time with his wife. Talking about what had happened in the past but, most important, how they could be there for each other in the future.

"Perfect timing, little one." Kate rubbed her gargantuan stomach—her words, not his. He was grateful for the way she looked. "I wanted our baby born in Texas so badly. I'll miss raising a family here."

"We'll be back on the ranch soon." He shook his head, baffled that his wife would continue to question his desire to run her family's ranch. "I'm done with being a Ranger, Kate. Really."

"I'm afraid you'll miss it." Her grip on his hand tightened, and tightened some more during the contraction.

This was one thing she was completely wrong about. He couldn't put his family in danger like that again, and he actually loved ranching. Even his father agreed it was time to live a normal life.

"I think you're supposed to breathe through those things, babe."

"Right. And don't call me babe. Oh, wow, here's another one."

Cord called for the nurse, who called for the doctor. They pushed, or Kate did and he held her hand. And sooner than he expected, he was a dad holding his brand-new baby boy.

"Looks like you've got that next-generation Ranger after

all," Kate said. "Guess he doesn't want to be called Lorna after his grandmother."

"I love you, Kathleen." Cord kissed his son's forehead, so thankful both of them were okay. "Whoever Danver Mc-Crea grows up to be, he'll always be protected by us both."

* * * * *

REQUEST YOUR FREE BOOKS!
2 FREE NOVELS PLUS 2 FREE GIFTS!

HARLEQUIN®

INTRIGUE®

BREATHTAKING ROMANTIC SUSPENSE

YES! Please send me 2 FREE Harlequin Intrigue® novels and my 2 FREE gifts (gifts are worth about $10). After receiving them, if I don't wish to receive any more books, I can return the shipping statement marked "cancel." If I don't cancel, I will receive 6 brand-new novels every month and be billed just $4.74 per book in the U.S. or $5.24 per book in Canada. That's a savings of at least 14% off the cover price! It's quite a bargain! Shipping and handling is just 50¢ per book in the U.S. and 75¢ per book in Canada.* I understand that accepting the 2 free books and gifts places me under no obligation to buy anything. I can always return a shipment and cancel at any time. Even if I never buy another book, the two free books and gifts are mine to keep forever.

182/382 HDN F42N

Name _____ (PLEASE PRINT) _____

Address _____ Apt. # _____

City _____ State/Prov. _____ Zip/Postal Code _____

Signature (if under 18, a parent or guardian must sign)

Mail to the **Harlequin® Reader Service:**
IN U.S.A.: P.O. Box 1867, Buffalo, NY 14240-1867
IN CANADA: P.O. Box 609, Fort Erie, Ontario L2A 5X3

**Are you a subscriber to Harlequin Intrigue books
and want to receive the larger-print edition?
Call 1-800-873-8635 or visit www.ReaderService.com.**

* Terms and prices subject to change without notice. Prices do not include applicable taxes. Sales tax applicable in N.Y. Canadian residents will be charged applicable taxes. Offer not valid in Quebec. This offer is limited to one order per household. Not valid for current subscribers to Harlequin Intrigue books. All orders subject to credit approval. Credit or debit balances in a customer's account(s) may be offset by any other outstanding balance owed by or to the customer. Please allow 4 to 6 weeks for delivery. Offer available while quantities last.

Your Privacy—The Harlequin® Reader Service is committed to protecting your privacy. Our Privacy Policy is available online at www.ReaderService.com or upon request from the Harlequin Reader Service.

We make a portion of our mailing list available to reputable third parties that offer products we believe may interest you. If you prefer that we not exchange your name with third parties, or if you wish to clarify or modify your communication preferences, please visit us at www.ReaderService.com/consumerschoice or write to us at Harlequin Reader Service Preference Service, P.O. Box 9062, Buffalo, NY 14269. Include your complete name and address.

HI13R

MURDER IN THE SMOKIES
by
Paula Graves

*When a string of murders rocks the small town of
Bitterwood, Detective Ivy Hawkins's gut tells her they are
all somehow connected. But no one believes her...except
for Sutton Calhoun, a man Ivy would much rather forget.*

Ivy closed the distance between them with deliberate steps.
"I thought you swore you'd never let the dust of Bitterwood
touch your feet again."

"That's a little melodramatic." Sutton laughed.

She shrugged. "You said it, not me."

True, he *had* said it. And meant it. And if Stephen Billings
hadn't walked into Cooper Security two weeks ago looking for help investigating his sister's murder, he probably
would've kept that vow without another thought.

He'd let himself forget Ivy and her uncomplicated friend-
ship. And if her cool gaze meant anything, whatever connection they'd shared fourteen years ago was clearly dead and
gone.

"I'm here on a job." He kept it vague.

"What kind of job?"

He should have known vague wouldn't work with a little
bulldog like Ivy Hawkins. She'd never been one to take no
for an answer. Maybe the truth was his best option.

"I'm here to look into a murder that happened here in Bitterwood a little over a month ago."

"April Billings," she said immediately.

He nodded. "Were you on that case?"

She shook her head. "She was the first."

Something about her tone tweaked his curiosity. "The first?"

"Murder," she said faintly. "First stranger murder in Bitterwood in twenty years."

"And you're sure it was a stranger murder?"

Her eyes met his, sharp and cautious. "All the signs were there."

"I thought you didn't investigate it."

"I didn't investigate it at the time it happened."

"But you've looked into her death since?"

She cocked her head slightly. "Who sent you to investigate this case? Are you with the TBI?"

He almost laughed at that thought. His father had had enough run-ins with the Tennessee Bureau of Investigation that both their faces were probably plastered to the Knoxville field office's front wall, right there with all the other most wanted. "No. Private investigation."

"You're a P.I.?" Her eyebrows arched over skeptical eyes.

"Sort of."

She was making him feel like a suspect. He didn't like it one bit.

Will Ivy and Sutton find the killer before
they become his next victims? Find out when
MURDER IN THE SMOKIES
hits shelves in June 2013, only from Harlequin Intrigue!

HARLEQUIN®

INTRIGUE®

WHEN A MOTHER'S LOVE MEETS A FATHER'S INSTINCT...

Ex-marine Adam Dalton once dreamed of a life with
Hadley O'Sullivan, but war and a near-fatal injury cost
him dearly. Now he returns to Dallas to discover
the unthinkable—Hadley is the prime suspect in the
disappearance of her twin baby girls...the daughters
he hadn't known he had. Despite their past, Adam and
Hadley know finding their children is their only hope to
finally becoming a family—if time doesn't run out first.

TRUMPED UP CHARGES

BY JOANNA WAYNE

Available May 21 from Harlequin® Intrigue®.

HI69693